THE LÖWENSKÖLD RING

Selma Lagerlöf

THE LÖWENSKÖLD RING

TRANSLATED BY LINDA SCHENCK

Norvik Press
1991

Other books in this series include:

Sigbjørn Obstfelder: *A Priest's Diary* (translated by James McFarlane)
Hjalmar Söderberg: *Short Stories* (translated by Carl Lofmark)
Bjørg Vik: *An Aquarium of Women* (translated by Janet Garton)
Annegret Heitmann (ed.): *No Man's Land. An Anthology of Modern Danish Women's Literature*
P.C. Jersild: *A Living Soul* (translated by Rika Lesser)
New Norwegian Plays (translated by Janet Garton and Henning Sehmsdorf)
Sara Lidman: *Naboth's Stone* (translated by Joan Tate)

Our logo is based on a drawing by Egil Bakka (University of Bergen) of a Viking ornament in gold foil, paper thin, with impressed figures (size 16 x 21 mm). It was found in 1897 at Hauge, Klepp, Rogaland, and is now in the collection of the Historisk museum, University of Bergen (inv.no.5392). It depicts a love scene, possibly (according to Magnus Olsen) between the fertility god Freyr and the maiden Gerðr; the large penannular brooch of the man's cloak dates the work as being most likely 10th century.

Cover illustration: *Interiör av en småländsk bondstuga* (Interior of a Swedish Peasant Cottage), by P. Hörberg. Photograph: Statens Konstmuseer, Stockholm. (Detail.)

British Library Cataloguing in Publication Data
Lagerlöf, Selma *1858–1940*
    The Löwensköld Ring
    I. Title
    839.736 [F]

ISBN 1-870041-14-3

First published in 1991 by Norvik Press, University of East Anglia, Norwich, NR4 7TJ, England
Managing Editors: James McFarlane and Janet Garton

Norvik Press has been established with financial support from the University of East Anglia, the Danish Ministry for Cultural Affairs, the Norwegian Cultural Department, and the Swedish Institute. Publication of this book has been aided by grants from the Swedish Institute and the Anglo-Swedish Literary Foundation.

Printed in Great Britain by the University of East Anglia, Norwich.

I

Oh, I know very well that in the old times there were many people who didn't know the meaning of fear. I've heard of lots of people who liked walking on the ice of a single cold night and who enjoyed nothing so much as riding behind horses known to bolt. There were even some who didn't mind playing a game of cards with Lieutenant Ahlegård, although they probably knew he was a card sharp and would always win. And I know of a few dauntless souls who were not afraid of beginning a journey on Friday or sitting down to a dinner table laid for thirteen. But I still wonder whether a single one of them would have had the courage to put on the terrible ring that once belonged to old General Löwensköld of Hedeby.

That same old General gave the Löwenskölds their name, property and title, and as long as any of them were still living at Hedeby his portrait hung between the windows in the large upstairs drawing room. The huge painting extended from floor to ceiling, and at first glance you took it to be no less than Charles the Twelfth himself, in a blue greatcoat and huge chamois gloves, his enormous cavalry boots placed firmly on the checkerboard floor; but when you moved closer you could see quite plainly that this was an entirely different kind of man.

A large, rough peasant face rose above the collar. The man in the painting appeared to have been born to follow the plough all the days of his life. Despite his ugliness, he looked sensible and dependable and decent. If he had come into the world in our times, he would no doubt have become at least a Justice of the Peace and Mayor of his town and — who knows? — he might even have been elected to Parliament. But as he lived in the days of the great hero king, he went to war as a poor soldier, returned as the famous General Löwensköld, and was rewarded for his service to the Crown with the manor of Hedeby in the parish of Bro.

In any case, the longer you looked at the painting, the more you accepted the man's appearance. You began to realize that this was what soldiers serving in the ranks of King Charles had looked like, the ones who had ploughed him a furrow through Poland and Russia. Not only adventurers and noblemen of the court had followed him; even simple, earnest fellows like the one in this portrait had loved him and found in him a king to live and die for.

As you contemplated the likeness of the old General there was usually some member of the Löwensköld family at hand to point out that no vanity had prompted the General to pull his left glove far enough down to expose the big signet ring on his index finger. He had been given that ring by the King — there was only one king for him — and the ring was in the portrait as a sign of Bengt Löwensköld's loyalty to him. After all, he had had to listen to bitter slander of his sovereign, hear people dare to claim that his imprudence and extravagance had brought the realm to the brink of ruin, yet the General had remained steadfast through it all. For

8

King Charles was a man the likes of whom the world had never known, and anyone who had attended upon him had learned that there were finer and nobler causes for which to take up arms than worldly glory and fortune.

Just as Bengt Löwensköld had wanted the royal ring in his portrait, he had also wanted to take it with him to the grave. Again, vanity had nothing to do with it. He did not mean to boast by wearing the ring of a great King on his finger when he entered the presence of Our Lord and the Archangels, but he may have hoped that when he stepped into the hall where Charles the Twelfth sat surrounded by all his swordsmen, the ring might serve as a token, so that even after death he would be allowed to remain near the man he had served and worshipped all his life.

And so when the coffin of the General was lowered into the vault he had had erected for himself in the churchyard at Bro, the ring was still on the index finger of his left hand. Many of those present grieved to see so fine a piece of jewellery be buried with a dead man, for the reputation of the General's ring was nearly as great as that of the man himself. People said that it was made of gold enough to purchase a farm, and that the red cornelian engraved with the initials of the King, with which it was set, was worth no less. Most people thought the General's sons had done an honourable thing in respecting their father's wish and letting him keep his treasure.

Now, if the General's ring really looked like the one in the painting, it was an ugly, cumbersome thing hardly anyone would want to wear today, but this doesn't prevent its having been greatly admired a couple of hundred years ago. For we must remember that almost all precious gems and objects of gold and silver had been surrendered to the Crown in those days of emergency currency and national bankruptcy, and that gold was something most people had heard of but never seen. This was why they were unable to forget the gold ring, lying under a coffin lid, where it did no good whatever. It almost seemed wrong to people that it was there. It could have been sold abroad for a vast sum, and bought bread for those who had nothing to live on but straw and bark.

Yet though there were many who might have wished they possessed the great treasure, no one seriously considered appropriating it. The ring was beneath the screwed-down coffin lid, in a bricked-up vault, beneath heavy stone slabs, inaccessible even to the boldest of thieves, and there, people thought, it must remain until the end of time.

II

In the month of March in 1741, Major General Bengt Löwensköld
had gone to his final resting place, and just a few months later in
the same year it came to pass that a little daughter of Captain
Göran Löwensköld, who was the eldest son of the General and
now lived at Hedeby, died of dysentery. She was buried on a
Sunday just after the morning service, and the whole congregation
joined the funeral procession to the Löwensköld tomb, where the
two huge tombstones had been upturned. The vault below them
had been opened by a mason so the little coffin of the dead child
could be placed next to that of her grandfather.

While the people were gathered at the tombside, listening to
the funeral service and eulogy, it's quite possible that some of
them happened to recall the royal ring, and lamented its being
buried in a grave where it benefited no one. Someone may even
have whispered to his neighbour that it should not be too difficult

to get at the ring now, since the vault would probably not be closed up until the next day.

One of the many people who stood there with these thoughts running through his mind was a farmer from Mellomstuga farm in the village of Olsby, by the name of Bård Bårdsson. He was by no means among those who had worried himself grey over the ring. On the contrary, whenever the ring was mentioned, all he said was that his farm was good enough for him and he would have no cause to begrudge the General's having taken even a bushel of gold with him to the tomb.

But standing in the cemetery he began, like so many others, to think how strange it was that the vault had been opened. Yet it did not please him. It made him unhappy. 'I do hope the Captain has it closed back up this very afternoon,' he thought. 'There are a lot of people who want to get at the ring.'

Although it was actually none of his business, he was increasingly preoccupied with the thought that there might be some risk involved in the vault's being left open over night. It was already August; the nights were dark, and if the vault were not closed up that very day a thief could sneak down there and abscond with the treasure.

He was seized with such anxiety that he considered approaching the Captain to warn him, but he knew very well people took him for a simpleton, and he had no desire to look the fool. 'I mean, you're quite right about all this,' he thought to himself, 'but if you meddle in it people will make a laughing stock of you. The Captain is such a sensible man, he's sure to have the hole bricked up.'

He was so engrossed in his thoughts he didn't even notice when the funeral service ended. He just stood at the tombside, and would have remained there if his wife had not pulled at his coat sleeve.

'What's the matter?' she asked. 'You're glued to this spot,

staring like a cat guarding a mousehole.'

Taken aback, the farmer looked up and found that he was alone with his wife in the churchyard.

'Oh, it's nothing,' he said. 'I was just wondering . . .'

He would have liked to tell his wife what he had been wondering about, but he realized that she was much more quick-witted than he. She would only say he was worrying over nothing. She would say that whether or not the vault was closed up was Captain Löwensköld's business, and his alone.

They turned homeward, and now that Bård Bårdsson had left the churchyard the thought of the vault should have left him, but it didn't. His wife chattered about the funeral: about the coffin and pallbearers, the procession and eulogy, and he added a word now and then so she wouldn't notice that he didn't remember a thing and hadn't heard a word. Soon his wife's voice was coming to him from a great distance. The same thought began running through his head again.

'Today is Sunday,' he said to himself, 'and the mason may not be willing to close up the vault on the Sabbath. But if he doesn't, the Captain could give the gravedigger a coin to guard the vault tonight. If only I could be sure he'd thought of it.'

Before he knew it, he was mumbling out loud. 'I should have gone up to the Captain. Shouldn't have minded people laughing at me.'

Completely oblivious of his wife walking beside him, he was only brought back to the present when she stopped in her tracks, staring at him.

'It's nothing really. I was just worrying about that same thing again,' he said.

And so they walked on, and were soon closing their door behind them.

At home he hoped his worries would leave him, and they probably would've if he'd been able to get down to work, but of course it was Sunday. After dinner was over the people at Mellomstuga went their separate ways. He was left sitting all alone, and soon began to fret again.

After a while he got up and went out and groomed his horse, with every intention of riding to Hedeby to have a word with the Captain. 'Otherwise the ring will probably be stolen tonight,' he thought.

But he never did. He was too timid. Instead, he went to a neighbouring farm to talk over his worries with the farmer, but as he did not find him alone he was once again too timid to speak. He returned home without having said anything.

He went to bed as soon as the sun set, determined to sleep until morning. But he couldn't sleep. He started to worry again, tossing and turning in bed.

This kept his wife awake, too. After a while she asked him what had him so worried.

'Nothing,' he replied as before. 'I'm just lying here wondering about something.'

'Well, I've heard that answer enough times today, and now I think I ought to be told what you're wondering about. Whatever's on your mind can't be so awful that you can't talk to me about it.'

When he heard these words from his wife, it occurred to Bård that he might be able to sleep if he took her advice.

'I'm only wondering whether they've closed up the General's vault,' he said, 'or if it's going to be open all night.'

His wife laughed. 'I've been wondering about that myself,' she said, 'and I suppose every single person who was at church today has thought about it, too. But I can't see it's anything for you to lose sleep over.'

Bård was glad to hear his wife take the matter so lightly. He felt better, and expected to fall asleep.

But as soon as he settled down, he started to worry once more. He saw shadows come sneaking from every direction and every house, every one with the same intent, heading for the churchyard and the open vault.

He tried to lie still so his wife would be able to sleep, but his head ached and he was sweating. He couldn't stop tossing and turning.

His wife lost patience and said, half in jest: 'My dear, I do think it would be better for you to go down to the church and have a look at the vault than to lie here tossing about without getting a wink of sleep.'

Hardly were the words out of her mouth before her husband jumped out of bed and began to dress. He thought his wife was quite right. It was only half an hour's walk from Olsby to the church at Bro. He would be back in an hour and then get a good night's sleep.

No sooner was he out the door than his wife realized how awful it would be for her husband to walk to the churchyard all alone, so she, too, jumped right out of bed and pulled on her clothes.

She caught up with him on the hill down from Olsby. Bård laughed when he heard her approaching.

'Coming along just to make sure I don't steal the General's ring?' he asked.

'Heaven forbid!' said his wife. 'Don't you think I know that you've no such thing in mind? I only came out to help, in case you run into the headless horseman or ghostly ghoul.'

They walked on quickly. Night had fallen and all the sky was dark except one narrow band of light in the west, but they knew the road very well. They chatted and were in high spirits, as they were only walking down to the churchyard to see if the vault was open, so Bård wouldn't have to lose any more sleep over it.

'It would be nigh on incredible if the Löwenskölds were so careless as not to seal up the ring,' said Bård.

'Well, we'll soon see,' said his wife. 'Goodness, we're alongside the churchyard wall already.'

Her husband stopped, surprised to hear his wife sounding so happy. Surely she didn't have any ulterior motives for this walk of theirs?

'Before we go in,' said Bård, 'I think we should agree upon what we'll do if the vault is open.'

'Closed or open, I can't see there'll be anything to do but go back home to bed.'

'No, I s'pose not. Right you are,' said Bård, moving on.

'We can't expect the gate to be open at this hour,' he said shortly.

'It won't be,' said his wife. 'We'll have to climb the wall if we're going to look in on the General and see how he is.'

Now her husband was in for another surprise. He heard the rattle of falling gravel and soon saw the figure of his wife outlined against the strip of light in the west. There she was, up on the wall. This was no acrobatic feat, as it was not very high, but it was still strange that she was keen enough to climb up first.

'Come on. I'll give you a hand up,' she said.

In a moment the wall was behind them and they were making their way cautiously and quietly among the little burial mounds.

Once Bård stumbled over a grave and nearly fell. It felt as if someone had been trying to trip him. Quaking with fright he said in a loud voice, so the dead could not mistake his intentions: 'I wouldn't like to be walking here with any wrongdoing in mind.'

'Neither would I,' said his wife. No question about it. Now, isn't that the vault over there?'

He could just make out the upturned slabs against the dark night sky.

A moment later they were at the tombside and found the vault open. The hole had not been closed up.

'What negligence,' he said. 'They've done this purely to subject anyone who knows what treasure is buried down here to the sorest temptation.'

'I suppose they trust that no one would dare cross the dead,' said his wife.

'I wouldn't like to go down into a vault like this,' he said. 'Jumping in would be all right, but then you'd be stuck down there like a fox in a pit.'

'I noticed this morning that there was a little ladder down into it,' said his wife, 'But they must at least have taken that away.'

'I'll just see about that,' said Bård, fumbling his way to the hole. 'Would you believe it?' he exclaimed. 'This is the limit. The ladder's still here!'

'How careless!' his wife agreed. 'Though I don't think it really matters. That man down there probably knows how to guard what's rightfully his.'

'If only I could be sure of it,' said her husband. 'Maybe I should at least take the ladder away.'

'I don't think we should touch anything,' said his wife. 'Tomorrow the gravedigger should find everything exactly as he left it today.'

They stood staring down into the hole, perplexed and undecided. And although they should have gone home now there was something mysterious, something neither of them dared put into words, keeping them there.

'I guess I could leave the ladder,' said Bård at last, 'if only I were certain the General had the power to keep thieves away.'

'You could go down there and see what power he has,' said his wife.

It was as if Bård had been waiting for his wife to say precisely that. In a trice he was on the ladder, on his way into the vault.

But no sooner had he dropped to the stone floor than he heard the ladder creak and found his wife coming down behind him.

'Following me down here as well?' he asked.

'I could hardly leave you alone with a dead man.'

'Ah, but I don't really think he'd do me any harm,' said her husband. 'I feel no cold hand trying to squeeze the life out of me.'

'No, he won't harm to us. He knows we don't mean to steal his ring,' said his wife. 'But of course things would be different if we started to unscrew the coffin lid, just to check.'

At once Bård fumbled his way to the General's coffin and began feeling along the edges. He located a screw with a little cross on the top.

'This is the perfect setup for a thief,' he said, carefully and skilfully beginning to unscrew the lid of the coffin.

'Don't you feel anything?' asked his wife. 'Don't you notice anything moving inside?'

'No, it's as quiet as the grave,' said her husband.

'He wouldn't be thinking we planned to deprive him of his most cherished possession,' said his wife. 'Things would be quite different if we took the lid off.'

'Well, you'll have to give me a hand with that,' said Bård.

They raised the lid, and now there was no curbing their craving for the treasure. They took the ring off the shrunken hand, replaced the lid, and without another word, crept back up. They held hands as they walked out through the graveyard, and not until they had climbed the low stone wall and were back on the road did they dare to speak.

'I'm beginning to think,' said his wife, 'that this was what he wanted. He's realized it's not right for a dead man to hold onto something so valuable, and so he gave it to us of his own free will.'

Her husband burst out laughing.

'That's a good one,' he said. 'You'll never convince me he let us take it of his own free will, but I don't suppose it was in his power to stop us.'

'Anyway,' said his wife, 'I think you've shown your mettle tonight. There aren't many men who would have gone down into the General's grave.'

'Well, I don't feel I've done anything wrong,' said Bård. 'I've never taken a penny from a living soul, but what does it matter if you take from a dead man something he doesn't need?'

Proud and pleased, they walked along. They were surprised no one else had thought of it. Bård said that as soon as he could he would go to Norway and sell the ring. They expected to get so much for it that their worries about money would be over forever.

'But,' said his wife, coming to a sudden halt, 'what's that I see? Can it already be sunrise? It's so light in the east!'

'It can't possibly be morning yet,' said the farmer. 'There must be a fire. Looks as if it's over Olsby way. It couldn't be . . .'

His wife's loud scream cut him short.

'It's our place that's on fire. Mellomstuga's on fire. The General's set fire to it. — '

On Monday morning, the gravedigger rushed straight over to Hedeby, which is quite near the church, to report that both he and the mason who was to close up the vault had thought the lid of the General's coffin looked askew and that the crests and coats-of-arms on it were in disarray.

An inspection was ordered forthwith. It was immediately apparent that the vault was in terrible disorder and the coffin screws were loose. When the lid was lifted off it could be seen at a glance that the royal ring was no longer where it belonged, on the General's left index finger.

III

I'm thinking about Charles XII and trying to comprehend how loved and feared he was.

I know that once, toward the end of his life, he walked into the church at Karlstad right in the middle of the service.

He'd come riding into town alone and with no one expecting him, and since he knew it was time for church, he tied his horse outside the church and went in through the main portal, just like anyone else.

The moment he walked through the door he saw that the parson was already at the pulpit, and so as not to interrupt the sermon, he stayed where he was, not even trying to find an aisle seat, but leaning against the doorpost and listening.

Although he had entered so quietly and although he remained in the shadows below the gallery, someone in the last pew recognized him. It may have been an old soldier who'd lost an arm or a leg and been shipped back home before the battle of Poltava who realized that the man with the brushed-back hair and aquiline nose must be the King. The moment he recognized him, he rose.

His neighbours in the pew must have wondered why, so he whispered to them that the King was in church. Without exception, one by one, everyone in the pew rose, as they did when the word of God was being read from the altar or the pulpit.

And so the news spread from pew to pew and they all, young and old, rich and poor, weak and strong, rose to their feet.

This was, as I've said, late in the life of King Charles, when his troubles and adversities had begun, and there may not have been a single person in church who had not lost one of his nearest and dearest or been deprived of his property on account of the King. If, by chance, there happened to be someone there with no grievance of his own to cherish, he only had to recall how impoverished his country was, how territories had been lost and the entire realm encircled by enemies.

But no matter, no matter. It took no more than a whisper that the man they had so often cursed was there in the house of God, to make them rise.

Standing they remained. No one considered sitting down. They couldn't. The King was standing by the church door, and as long as he was standing, they all had to stand. To sit down would have been to show disrespect for the King.

Perhaps it would be a long sermon, but they'd have to endure it. They couldn't fail the man over by the door.

Being a King and soldier, he was accustomed to his men unquestioningly going to their deaths for him. But in this church he was surrounded by simple townspeople and artisans, common Swedish men and women who had never stood to attention on command. Yet all he need do was appear among them and they were in his power. They would have followed him anywhere, given him anything, they believed in him, idolized him. Throughout the church they thanked God for the man of miracles who was

21

Sweden's King.

As I said, I am trying to imagine all this in order to see how the love of King Charles could fill someone's whole being, take such a firm hold on a gruff and grumbling old heart that everyone expected it to remain there, even after death. —

In truth, after it was discovered that the General's ring had been stolen, what surprised the people of Bro parish most was that anyone had been bold enough to commit the deed. They said that thieves could more easily have robbed a woman in love, buried with her engagement ring on her finger. Or that if a mother had had a lock of her child's hair in her hand on her deathbed there would have been less to fear in taking it from her. Or that if a pastor had had his Bible as a pillow in his coffin it could probably have been stolen without the criminal coming to harm. But to steal the ring of Charles XII from the finger of the late General of Hedeby was an undertaking it was impossible to imagine any man of woman born attempting.

Of course investigations were made, but the criminal was not revealed. The thief had come and gone in the dead of night, leaving not a clue for the searchers to follow.

Once again, people were surprised. Ghosts had been known to walk night after night, to single out the perpetrators of far smaller crimes.

Later, though, when it became clear that the General had by no means left his ring to its destiny, but had fought to repossess it with the same grim ruthlessness he would have shown if the ring had been stolen from him in this life, no one was in the least surprised. No one doubted it in the slightest, for this was precisely what they had expected.

IV

Several years after the disappearance of the General's ring, the parson from Bro was called one day to the deathbed of Bård Bårdsson, a poor farmer from Olsby, who insisted that he must see the parson before he died. The parson was an elderly man, and when he heard that he had been called to see a sick man who lived deep in the distant forest, he proposed that his curate go instead, but the dying man's daughter who had brought her father's message, said that it had to be the parson or no one at all. Her father had told her to say that he had something to tell the parson that no one else in the world could know.

When the parson heard this he began to ransack his memory. Bård Bårdsson had been a good man. Something of a simpleton, of course, but this was scarcely something for him to worry about on his deathbed. No, by human reckoning the parson thought he was a man with a debt to collect from our Lord. Over the last seven years he had been beset with every conceivable sort of suffering and misfortune. His farm burned down, his cattle died of disease or were killed off by wild animals, the frost ravaged his fields, and he was now as poor as Job. In the end, his wife, driven to desperation by all their misfortunes, had drowned herself. Bård had moved to their distant mountain pasture, the last of his possessions. Since then neither he nor his children had been to church. Whether or not they were still living in the parish had been the subject of much speculation at the parsonage.

'Knowing your father, I think his crimes are no worse than they can be confessed to my curate,' said the parson, giving Bårdsson's daughter a benevolent smile.

She was a girl of fourteen, big and strong for her age. Her face was broad and her features coarse. Like her father, she looked a little simple-minded, but childish innocence and honesty brightened her face.

'It wouldn't be fear of Big Bengt, would it, Sir, that was keeping you from coming to our place?'

'What do you mean, my dear child?' the parson replied. 'Who is this Big Bengt?'

'Why, he's the one who's made things so hard for us.'

'Oh, I see,' said the parson, 'I see. So he's a man called Big Bengt, is he?'

'Didn't you know, Sir, that he was the one who set fire to Mellomstuga?'

'No, no one ever told me,' said the parson.

But he got right up out of his chair and began to pack his psalter and a little wooden chalice he always took along on parish visits.

'He was the one who drove my mother to her death,' the girl went on.

'How dreadful, my dear,' said the pastor. 'Is this man you call Big Bengt still alive? Have you seen him?'

'No, I've never seen him, but he's still alive, that's for sure. It

24

was because of him we had to move to the mountains and the wild woods. And there he's left us well nigh alone until last week, when Father cut his foot with the axe.'

'And do you mean to tell me that Big Bengt was to blame for that?' the parson asked softly, as he hurried to open the door, and called to the farmhand to saddle his horse.

'Father said that if Big Bengt hadn't cast a spell on the axe, he would never have hurt himself. It wasn't a deep cut either, but today Father saw that gangrene had set in. He said Big Bengt had done him in and now he must die, and so he sent me to the parsonage to ask you to come, Sir, just as quickly as ever you could.'

'And indeed I shall,' said the parson. He had pulled on his riding cloak and hat as the girl spoke. 'But I just can't understand, my dear,' he said, ' why this Big Bengt is so cruel to him. Do you suppose your father once did him some wrong?'

'I do,' said the child. 'And my father doesn't deny it, though he's never said what it was, neither to me nor my brother. But I think, Sir, that's what he wants to tell you now.'

'Well, if that's the case then we cannot hasten to him quickly enough.' He had now pulled on his riding gloves, and he and the girl walked out and mounted their horses.

The parson hardly said a word during the whole ride to the mountain pasture. He just sat thinking over the remarkable things the girl had told him. He personally had only met one man known as Big Bengt. But then again, this might not be the man the girl had been talking about. She might have been talking about someone quite different.

As he approached the little farm, a young man, Bård Bårdsson's son Ingilbert, came toward him. He was a few years older than his sister, big like her and with features like hers, but his eyes were deeper set and he looked less open and friendly.

'You've had a long journey here, Sir,' he said as he helped him to dismount.

'I suppose I have,' said the old man, 'but it went more quickly than I expected.'

'I would have fetched you myself, Sir,' said Ingilbert, 'but I've been out fishing since last night. I've only just come home and heard about the gangrene in Father's foot and your having been sent for.'

'Don't worry. Märta's been as good as any man,' said the parson. 'But how's your father?'

'I think he's pretty poorly, Sir, but his mind is quite clear. He was relieved to hear I'd seen you coming out of the wood.'

So the parson went inside to see Bård, and the children sat waiting on the rocky outcrop outside the cottage. They spoke solemnly about their dying father. They said he'd always been good to them. But he had never been happy since the day Mellomstuga burned down, and so it was best for him to leave this life behind.

At one point the girl mentioned that their father must have something on his conscience.

'Him?' said her brother. 'What could be troubling him? I've never seen him lift a hand against man or beast.'

'But still, there was something he wanted to tell the parson and no one else.'

'Did he say that?' asked Ingilbert. 'Did he say there was something he wanted to tell the parson before he died? I thought he just wanted him to come and give him a last communion.'

'When he sent me off today he told me to ask the parson to come personally. He said there was no one else in the whole world to whom he could confess his terrible sin.'

Ingilbert sat thinking a moment. 'That's an odd one,' he said. 'I wonder if it might not be something he's imagined, all alone up here, like those stories he's always telling about Big Bengt. I think he's dreamt it all up.'

'Big Bengt was what he wanted to talk to the parson about,' said the girl.

'I'll bet it's all a pack of lies,' said Ingilbert.

He rose suddenly and went to a shutter that was open to let a little air and light in through a hole in the wall of the house, which had no proper windows. The sick man's bed was so close to the shutter that Ingilbert could hear every word he said, and the son listened to his father's words without the slightest scruple. Perhaps he'd never even heard that it was wrong to eavesdrop on a confession. In any case, he was convinced that his father had no dark secrets to reveal.

After he had stood at the shutter a while, he went back to his sister.

'What did I tell you?' he began. 'Father's telling the parson that Mother and he stole the royal ring from old General Löwensköld.'

'God have mercy on us then!' his sister exclaimed. 'Shouldn't we tell the parson it's a lie, just something he's making up?'

'We can't do anything now,' said Ingilbert. 'I suppose Father may say whatever he chooses now. We'll have to talk to the parson afterwards.'

He stood stealthily by the shutter for a few minutes, and then returned to his sister.

'Now he's saying that the very night he and Mother had stolen the ring from the grave, Mellomstuga burned down. He says it was the General who set fire to the house.'

'You can hear he's dreaming it up,' said his sister. 'If he's told us once he's told us a hundred times, it was Big Bengt who set fire to Mellomstuga.'

Ingilbert was back at his post by the shutter before the words were out of her mouth. He stood there and harkened for a long time, and when he went back to his sister again, his face was quite grey.

'He says the General brought down all this misery upon him,

to make him return the ring. He says Mother was frightened and wanted them to go to the Captain at Hedeby and give him the ring, and Father would have been more than happy to do so if he'd durst, but he feared they'd both be hanged if they admitted having stolen from a dead man. But then Mother couldn't stand it and so she went and drowned herself.'

At this his sister, too, paled with horror.

'But,' she said, 'Father always said it was . . . '

'Of course. He just explained to the parson that he never dared tell anyone who had brought these troubles down upon his head. He only told us children, because we were too young to know what he meant, that a man called Big Bengt was persecuting him. He said the country people had always called the General Big Bengt.'

Märta Bårdsdotter slumped over. 'Then it must be true,' she whispered, as quietly as if it were her last breath.

She looked round. The farm was at the edge of a mountain pool, with dark, wooded cliffs rising all around. No human dwelling in sight, no one to run to. Nothing but great, irrevocable solitude.

And in the shade of the trees she imagined the dead man standing, ready to send misfortune down upon them.

Being the kind of child she was, she had no real sense of the shame and disgrace her parents had brought on themselves, but what she did understand was this: that a spectre, an implacable, omnipotent being from the land of the dead, was persecuting them all. She expected him to make himself visible at any moment, and she was so frightened her teeth were chattering.

It struck her that her father had been living with this selfsame terror in his soul for seven years. She was fourteen now and she knew she had only been seven when Mellomstuga burned down. Her father had known all the time that the dead man was out to get him. For him, it would be a release to die.

'You don't believe it, though, do you, Ingilbert?' she asked, in a last effort to stave off her terror.

But then she saw that Ingilbert's hands were shaking and his eyes were wide with fear. He was frightened too, just as frightened as she.

'What am I to believe?' Ingilbert whispered. 'Father says he's been on the point of leaving for Norway a number of times to sell the ring, but that he's never been able to get away. Once he was taken ill, another time his horse broke its leg just as he was about to leave the farm.'

'What does the parson say?' asked his sister.

'He asked Father why he kept the ring all these years, since it was so hazardous to possess. But Father replied that he thought the Captain would have him hanged if he admitted to his crime. He had no choice but to keep it. But now he knew he was dying, and so he wanted to give the ring to the parson and have it returned to the General in his grave, so the curse would be lifted from us children and we could move back down to the village.'

'I'm glad the parson's here,' said the girl. 'I don't know what I'll do when he's gone. I'm so frightened. I keep thinking the General's standing over there under the pines. Imagine his having been here all this time, watching us! And Father may even have seen him.'

'I think Father probably has seen him,' said Ingilbert.

He went back to the cottage to listen. When he returned, the look in his eyes had changed.

'I've seen the ring,' he said. 'Father gave it to the parson. It shone like a flame, red and yellow. It glowed. The parson looked at it and said he knew it to be the General's ring. Go over by the shutter and have a look!'

'I'd rather hold a viper in my hand than look at that ring!' said the girl. 'You can't mean it's a beautiful sight?'

Ingilbert looked away.

'I know that it's been our undoing,' he said. 'Still, I liked it.'

Just as Ingilbert was saying this the stern, loud voice of the parson could be heard from within. He had allowed the sick man to speak his piece. Now it was his turn.

Naturally, the parson could not possibly take all this wild talk about being pursued by the dead at face value. He tried to explain to the farmer that he was suffering the wrath of God for having committed such a heinous crime as robbing a corpse. Nor could the parson concede that the General could have the power to cause fires or afflict man or beast with illness. No, all the suffering to which Bård had been subjected was God's way of compelling him to repent and return the stolen goods while he was still alive, so that his sins would be forgiven and he could enter the Kingdom of Heaven.

Old Bård Bårdsson lay still, listening to the parson's speech without protest. Yet it didn't appear to convince him. He had been through too many horrors to believe that they were all the work of the Lord.

But the young people, sitting there trembling for fear of ghosts and spirits, brightened.

'Did you hear that?' said Ingilbert, clutching tight to his sister's arm. 'Did you hear the parson say it wasn't the General?'

'Yes,' said his sister. She was sitting there with her hands folded, taking every one of the parson's words to heart.

Ingilbert rose, inhaled deeply, and straightened up. His fear had left him and he was a new man. He strode quickly to the door of the little house and entered.

'What is it?' asked the parson.

'I want a word with Father.'

'Get out. Right now I am talking to your father,' said the parson sternly.

He turned back to Bård Bårdsson, speaking sometimes with authority, sometimes gently and compassionately.

Ingilbert had sat down on the stone slab and buried his face in his hands. But he was overcome with anguish. He went into the cottage a second time, and was once again dismissed.

When it was all over, Ingilbert was to guide the parson back through the woods. All went well at first, but after a while they had to cross a marsh on a narrow path of logs. The parson didn't remember this from the ride out. He asked Ingilbert if they had gone astray, but Ingilbert replied that this was a short cut and would save them a great many miles.

The parson looked sharply at Ingilbert, thinking that he, like his father, seemed to be possessed by a craving for gold. He recalled that Ingilbert had gone in and out of the cottage repeatedly, as if to keep his father from giving up the ring.

'This path is narrow and dangerous, Ingilbert,' said the parson. 'I am afraid my horse will lose his footing on these slippery logs.'

'If I lead him, Sir, you'll have nothing to fear,' said Ingilbert, grabbing the horse's reins. But out in the middle of the marsh, with nothing but quagmire on either side, Ingilbert began to urge the parson's horse backwards, as if he were trying to force it off the narrow path.

The horse reared and the parson, who was nearly unseated, shouted to the young man for God's sake to drop the reins.

But Ingilbert did not appear to hear. The parson saw him, face dark and teeth clenched, struggling to force the horse down into the marsh. It would have been certain death for both horse and rider.

Then the parson pulled a little goatskin pouch out of his pocket. He threw it straight at Ingilbert's face.

The young man dropped the reins to catch the pouch, and the horse was freed. He bolted down the path. Ingilbert was left behind, and made no effort to follow.

V

After such rough usage, it wasn't surprising the parson felt a bit giddy, and that it was evening before he was able to make his way back down to the village. Nor was it to be wondered at that he didn't emerge from the woods on the Olsby road, which was the best and most direct route, but had turned too far south and come out right above Hedeby.

As he rode around deep in the forest, he thought that the first thing he should do when he had made his way home was send for the sheriff and ask him to go up into the woods and retrieve the ring from Ingilbert. But since he now happened to be passing by Hedeby, he held a little council with himself as to whether he shouldn't turn in there and tell Captain Löwensköld just who had made so bold as to go down into the vault and steal the royal ring.

One might think it unnecessary for him to ponder at length on such a natural matter, but the parson hesitated because he knew the Captain and his father had not always seen eye to eye. The Captain was as much a man of peace as his father had been a man of war. He had hastened to retire from active service as soon as peace had been made with the Russians, and since then had devoted all his time to the welfare of the nation, which had been shattered during the war years. He was against absolutism and the glories of war and, yes, he often spoke ill of Charles XII himself, as he did of so many other things the old man had prized. And to add insult to injury, the son had been an activist in the Parliamentary War, but always on the side of the pacifists. Yes, he and his father had had grounds enough for dispute.

When the General's ring had been stolen seven years earlier, the parson and many like him had felt that the Captain made too little effort to recover it. All this now made him think: 'It's no good my bothering to dismount here at Hedeby. The Captain couldn't care less whether the royal ring is on his father's finger or on Ingilbert's. I'd better just report the theft to Sheriff Carelius.'

But then, just as the parson was deliberating the matter, he saw the gate that marked the way to Hedeby swing very slowly out and stay wide open.

Although this was something of a strange sight, there are gates that open on their own like that if they are not properly closed, and the parson was not disturbed. He did, however, take it as a sign that he ought to ride down to Hedeby.

The Captain received him cordially, rather more so than was his custom.

'How nice of you to drop in, dear fellow,' he said. 'In fact, I've been wanting to see you, and was about to come down to the parsonage earlier today, to have a word with you about a rather odd event.'

'Well, my dear Löwensköld, that would have been a waste of your time,' said the parson. 'Early this morning I was sent for from Olsby, on the other side of the parish, to administer the last rites, and I am only now returning. It's been an adventuresome day for an old man like me.'

'I can say the same, although I've hardly been out of my chair. I assure you, my friend, that though I am a man of nearly fifty, and have seen a great deal during the terrible war years and since, nothing so peculiar has ever happened to me as what I've experienced today.'

'In that case,' said the parson, 'tell me about it, Löwensköld, my friend. I've also got an exceptional tale to tell you. Yet I wouldn't claim it's the most remarkable thing that has ever befallen me.'

'Ah well,' said the Captain. 'It may very well be that you'll find nothing at all strange in my tale. That was exactly what I wanted to ask you. — You've heard of Gathenhielm, haven't you?'

'The horrible pirate and savage privateer who was made an admiral by King Charles? Who hasn't heard of him?'

'Well, at our midday meal,' the Captain continued, 'we happened to be speaking of the war. My sons and their tutor started asking all sorts of questions about those days — I'm sure you've noticed that young people are always asking about those disastrous war years, and how they never ask a thing about the terrible years we Swedes had to go through after the death of King Charles, when the war and the empty treasury left us ruined. My God, what little credit they give us for rebuilding fire-ravaged towns, setting up factories and mills, clearing and replanting. I do believe my sons are ashamed of me and my contemporaries because we ceased going on campaigns and laying foreign lands to waste. They seem to think this makes us less manly than our fathers, and that the Swedish vigour of former times has abandoned us.'

'You're quite right about that,' said the parson. 'The love of the young for things martial is indeed deplorable, Löwensköld my friend.'

'At any rate, I tried to satisfy their wish to hear of a great military hero by telling them about Gathenhielm and his brutal treatment of merchants and peaceable wayfarers, expecting the story to fill them with horror and disgust. And, in fact, it did so. Then I bade them consider that this Gathenhielm was a real son of the war years, and I asked them if they would choose to see the world peopled with such reprehensible creatures.

But before my sons could reply, their tutor began to speak, requesting that I allow him to relate another story about Gathenhielm. Since he claimed this adventure would confirm what I'd already said about his unbridled savagery, I gave my consent.

His story was about when Gathenhielm died, at an early age, and his body was interred in Onsala church in a marble sarcophagus he had stolen from the King of Denmark. From then on, the church was beset by so many ghosts that the parishioners grew desperate. There was no other solution than to dig up the body and bury it on a deserted island far out at sea. They did so, and peace returned to the church, but fishermen who approached Gathenhielm's new resting place reported that a terrible crashing and commotion could always be heard, and that the foam was forever breaking high across the poor little island. The fishermen said all the sailors and tradesmen Gathenhielm had had thrown overboard from ships he had captured must be arising from their watery graves to harass and torment him, and they did everything they could to avoid sailing past there. Still, one dark night a fisherman chanced to pass too close by the hazardous island. He felt himself being drawn into a whirlwind, the waves lashed at his face and a booming voice called to him: "Go to Gata in Onsala and tell my wife to send me seven bundles of hazelwood switches and two juniper rods".'

Although the parson had listened patiently to the tale, when it became clear to him that his neighbour had nothing but a common ghost story to tell, he could hardly suppress a gesture of impatience. But the Captain paid no heed.

'Of course, my dear fellow, there was nothing to do but respond to this command. And Gathenhielm's wife did obey. The strongest of hazel switches and the thickest of juniper rods were made ready, and one of the Onsala men rowed out to sea with them.'

This time the parson made such a clear attempt to interrupt, that the Captain noticed his impatience.

'I know what you're thinking, my friend,' he said, 'as I had the same thoughts at dinner, listening to the tale, but now I beg you to hear me out. I would just like to add that the man from Onsala must have been resolute and devoted to his master, or he would hardly have accomplished his mission. When he approached the burial place, the waves were crashing over it as if there had been a great storm, and the uproar and commotion could be heard far and wide. But the man rowed as close as he could, and managed to throw the bundles of switches and the juniper rods onto the island. He then rowed hastily away from that terrible place.'

'My dear fellow . . .' the parson began, but the Captain was implacable.

'He didn't row very far, however, before resting on the oars to see if anything extraordinary would happen. Nor did he wait in vain. For the foam at once rose sky high above the island, with a din like the thunder of a battlefield and dreadful cries of distress from across the water. This went on for some time and then began to lessen, until at last the waves completely ceased storming Gathenhielm's grave. It was soon as still and calm there as anywhere else. As the man raised the oars to turn homeward, a booming, triumphant voice called to him:

"Go to Gata in Onsala and tell my wife that, dead or alive, Lasse Gathenhielm defeats his enemies".'

The parson had sat listening, his head bowed. Now that the story was over, he looked questioningly up at the Captain.

'As the tutor concluded his tale,' said the Captain, 'I could see quite plainly that my sons sympathized with that rogue Gathenhielm and enjoyed hearing of his arrogance. So I remarked that although it was a well-made tale, the story could hardly be anything but a lie. "Because," said I, "if a crude pirate like Gathenhielm is supposed to have had the power to defend himself even after death, then how do you explain my father? He was every bit as much a thunderer as Gathenhielm and, moreover, a good and honest man, but he allowed a thief to force his way into his vault and rob him of the thing he held dearest, and he did not have the power to prevent it at the time or to pursue the guilty man in any way since".'

At these words the parson rose with uncommon haste.

'That's exactly what I was thinking about,' said he.

'Then just wait until you hear what happened next,' the Captain went on. 'No sooner had I said these words when I heard a loud moan behind my chair. It sounded so much like my late father, the way he used to groan and sigh in his old age, that I thought he was standing there behind me, and I leapt to my feet. There was no one to be seen, but I was so sure it was his voice I had heard that I could not return to the table. I've been sitting here all alone ever since, thinking about it. And I would set great store by your thoughts on the subject, my dear friend. Was it my father I heard, lamenting his lost treasure? If I thought he were still yearning for it, I would rather go searching far and wide than have him spend one more moment in the cruel distress to which that moan bore witness.'

'This is the second time today I have been asked whether the dead General is still grieving for his lost ring and wishing for it back,' said the parson. 'With your permission, dear friend, I shall begin by telling my tale, after which we two shall exchange views.'

And so the parson told his tale, noting to himself that there had been no need to fear that the Captain would not champion his father's cause. The parson had not realized how even the most peaceable man is aroused when an injustice is perpetrated against his father. He now saw the veins in the Captain's face swelling, his fists clenching so the knuckles went white. A terrible fury had possessed him.

Of course the parson told it in his own way. He explained how the wrath of God had afflicted the evil-doers, and he was not a bit prepared to admit that the dead man had intervened.

But the Captain interpreted it all differently. He saw that his father had not been able to find peace in his grave because the ring had been taken from his index finger. He felt anguish and pangs of conscience because he had taken the matter all too lightly until now. It was like a piercing, throbbing wound in his heart.

The parson saw how upset the Captain was, and was almost afraid to admit that the ring had been taken from him, but this news was received with a sort of grim satisfaction.

'I am glad to hear that one of the gang of thieves is still alive and just as despicable as the others were,' said Captain Löwensköld. 'The General has struck the fellow's parents, and struck hard. Now it's my turn.'

The parson noted the implacable harshness in his voice and grew increasingly concerned. He feared the Captain would strangle Ingilbert with his own hands, or flog him to death.

'I thought it my duty to deliver the dead man's message to you, Löwensköld, my friend,' said the parson, 'but I hope you will not be too rash. My next step will be to inform the sheriff of the theft that has been committed against my person.'

'Please yourself on that account, my friend,' said the Captain. 'But I assure you, you needn't trouble, as I shall deal with the matter personally.'

After this the parson knew there was nothing to be gained in remaining at Hedeby. He rode off as soon as he could, hoping to get a message to the sheriff by nightfall.

But Captain Löwensköld summoned all his men together, told them what had happened, and asked them to go with him the next morning and capture the thief. No one refused him and the late General this service, and the remainder of the evening was spent searching for all kinds of weapons — old blunderbusses, short spears, long rapiers, cudgels and scythes.

VI

No fewer than fifteen men followed the Captain at four o'clock the next morning to hunt down the thief, and the fighting spirit ran high. They had a just cause and, in addition, the General behind them. They trusted that since the dead man had pursued the matter this far, he would no doubt see it through to a successful conclusion.

Now, the real wilderness did not begin for some five miles past Hedeby. To begin with they crossed a wide valley, cultivated in places and dotted with small barns. Clusters of buildings could be seen here and there on the hilltops. Olsby, the village where Bård Bårdsson's farm had been until the General burned it down, was among them.

Beyond this was the great forest, covering a vast expanse, blanketing the ground with tree after endless tree. But they had not yet passed the last trace of human endeavour. There were narrow paths through the woods leading to summer pastures and charcoal-making sites.

The appearance and stature of the Captain and his followers somehow changed when they entered the great forest. They had traversed these parts before, hunting game, and the thrill of the chase rose in them. They began casting sharp glances into the undergrowth, and moving lightly and stealthily.

'Let's agree on one point, men,' said the Captain. 'None of you is to come to grief over the thief. Leave him to me. All I ask of you is, don't let him get away!'

That order would probably not have been obeyed. The same men who, only recently, had peaceably gone about the business of hanging the hay on the hayricks, were now burning with the desire to give that thief Ingilbert a lesson he'd never forget.

But they got no farther than the part of the forest where the great pines, there since time immemorial, were so thick they made a ceiling above them, where the underbrush ceased and only moss covered the ground, when they caught sight of three men approaching, carrying between them a litter of lashed boughs, on which a fourth man lay.

The Captain and his party hastened toward them, and the bearers stopped at the sight of so many men. They had covered the face of the man on the litter with big fern leaves, so no one could see who he was, but the men from Hedeby still thought they knew, and a chill ran down their spines.

They didn't see the old General standing by the litter. Oh, no. Not so much as a glimpse of him. And yet they knew he was there. He had come down out of the woods with the dead man. He was standing there, pointing a finger at him.

The three litter bearers were good men, well-known in these parts. There was Erik Ivarsson who had a big farm at Olsby, and his brother Ivar Ivarsson who, having never married, lived as a member of Erik's family, on the farm where they both grew up. The two of them were getting on in years, while the third member

41

of their company was a young man. He, too, was known to all. His name was Paul Eliasson and he was the Ivarssons' foster son.

The Captain approached the Ivarssons, and they set down the litter to shake hands in greeting, but the Captain ignored their outstretched hands. His eyes were fixed on the fern leaves covering the man's face.

'Is this Ingilbert Bårdsson?' he asked in a strange, harsh voice. It was as if the question came out involuntarily.

'Yes.' said Erik Ivarsson, 'But how did you know, Captain? Did you recognize his clothes?'

'No,' said the Captain, 'I didn't recognize his clothes. I haven't seen him for five years.'

Both his own men and the newcomers glanced curiously at the Captain. They all found something strange and frightening about him that morning. He was not himself. He was not the pleasant, polite man he usually was.

He began questioning the Ivarssons. What were they doing in the woods at that early hour, and where had they found Ingilbert? The Ivarssons were respectable farmers and disliked having questions fired at them like this, but he succeeded in getting the essentials out of them.

The day before they had carried some food and flour up to the herders at their mountain pasture, some ten miles further into the forest, and had stayed the night. Early that morning they had started homeward, Ivar Ivarsson marching ahead of the other two. Ivar Ivarsson had been a soldier, and knew how to pace his strides. He was a difficult man to keep up with.

When Ivar Ivarsson was quite far ahead he had seen a man approaching him on the path. The woods were wide open there. No bushes, just tree trunks, and he had seen the man at quite a distance, though he'd not been able to identify him immediately. Clouds of mist hovered between the trees, and when the sunlight caught them they turned to yellow haze. You could see through them somewhat, but not perfectly clearly.

Ivar Ivarsson had noticed that when the man caught sight of him he stopped in great terror and stretched out his arms to ward him off. And when Ivar had moved a few steps forward, the man had fallen to his knees, shouting out that he should come no closer. It seemed the man had taken leave of his senses, and Ivar Ivarsson wanted to rush up and help him, but the man rose and fled into the woods. But he only ran a few paces. Suddenly he dropped headlong and lay motionless. By the time Ivar Ivarsson reached him, he was already dead.

Ivar Ivarsson had recognized the man by now as Ingilbert Bårdsson, son of the Bård Bårdsson who had once lived in Olsby but moved to his mountain pasture after his house burned down and his wife drowned. He couldn't understand how Ingilbert could fall down dead, when no hand had touched him, and he tried vainly to shake him back to life. When the others caught up they saw immediately he was dead. The Bårdssons having been their neighbours at Olsby, they could not just leave Ingilbert in the woods, so they made a litter and carried him.

The Captain stood listening to this with a grim expression. It seemed true enough. Ingilbert was dressed as if for a long journey, a rucksack on his back and shoes on his feet. The spear on the litter must have been his as well. He had undoubtedly been on his way to sell the ring abroad, but when he met Ivar Ivarsson deep in the forest he had imagined he was seeing the spectre of the General. Of course. That was it. Ivar Ivarsson was wearing an old soldier's coat and the brim of his hat was turned up like a Caroline's. The distance, the mist and a guilty conscience accounted for the mistake.

But the Captain was still displeased. By now he was feeling bloodthirsty. He wanted to crush the life out of Ingilbert Bårdsson with his own strong arms. He needed an outlet for revenge, and none was forthcoming.

Yet even he could see that this was unreasonable, and he pulled himself together and explained to the Ivarssons why he and his men had set out that morning. He added that he wished to find out if the dead man still had the ring on his person.

In his present mood, he hoped the men from Olsby would refuse, and make him fight for his rights. But they found his request quite reasonable and moved aside while two of the Captain's men searched the dead man's pockets, his shoes, his pack, every stitch of his clothing.

To begin with the Captain paid close attention to the search, but once, when he happened to glance toward the farmers, it seemed to him they were exchanging mocking looks, as if they were certain he would find nothing.

Which was exactly what happened. They had to abandon the search without finding the ring. At this the Captain's suspicions naturally turned on the farmers. So did his men's. Where had the ring gone? Ingilbert must have had it when he fled. Where was it now?

No one saw the General now, either, but they sensed his presence. He was among them, pointing at the three men from Olsby. They had it.

It was very possible they had searched the dead man's pockets and found the ring.

It was also possible the story they had just told was not true, and that things had happened differently. These men were from the same area as the Bårdssons and might have known they had the ring. They might have heard of Bård's death and realized, when they met his son in the woods, that he intended to run off with the ring, so they could have attacked and killed him to acquire the treasure for themselves.

There were no signs of bloodshed other than a graze on Ingilbert's forehead. The Ivarssons had said that he'd hit his head on a stone as he fell, but wasn't it possible that the graze had been

44

made by the broad cudgel Paul Eliasson had in his hand?

The Captain stood looking down. A battle was raging inside him. He had heard nothing but good spoken of the three men, and he was loathe to believe they had murdered and robbed.

All his men had gathered around him. A couple of them stood poised, brandishing their weapons. No one expected to leave without a fight.

Then Erik Ivarsson stepped up to the Captain. 'Both of us brothers, and Paul Eliasson who is our foster son and soon to become my son-in-law, have some idea of what you and your men must be thinking. Captain, we do not want to part without giving you the opportunity to search our pockets and clothing as well.'

This offer put the Captain's mind more at ease. He protested. Both the Ivarssons and their foster son were above suspicion.

But the farmers wanted the matter cleared up. They began emptying their own pockets and removing their shoes, so the Captain gestured to his men to let them have their way.

No ring was found, but in Ivar Ivarsson's birchbark rucksack they found a little goatskin pouch.

'Does this pouch belong to you?' the Captain asked, when he had examined it and found it empty.

If Ivar Ivarsson had simply said 'yes' that might have been the end of the matter, but instead he made an admission, as calmly as could be.

'No, it was on the path not far from where Ingilbert fell. The pouch looked useful and in good condition, so I put it in my pack.'

'But this was the very same kind of pouch the ring was in when the parson threw it to Ingilbert,' said the Captain, the grimness returning to both his voice and features. 'And so I think you Ivarssons will have to come along to the sheriff, unless you prefer to turn the ring over of your own free will.'

The men from Olsby now lost patience.

'You have no right to threaten us with arrest, Captain,' said

45

Erik Ivarsson. He grasped the spear lying by Ingilbert to force his way through; his brother and son-in-law came to his side.

At first the men from Hedeby stood back in surprise, all but the Captain who chuckled with delight at having an outlet for his fury. He drew his sabre and slashed the spear in two.

This was the only feat of arms performed in that particular war. The Captain's own men pulled him back and wrenched his weapon from him.

For the fact was that Sheriff Carelius had also found a reason to take a turn in the great forest that morning. Followed by a deputy, he had appeared on the path at exactly the right moment.

There were more investigations and cross-examinations, but the final result was still that Erik Ivarsson, his brother Ivar and their foster son Paul were arrested and detained, under firm suspicion of theft and manslaughter.

VII

It cannot be denied that in Värmland in those days our forests were wide and our fields small, the farmyards large but the cottages cramped, the roads narrow but the hills steep, the doorways low but the thresholds high, the churches humble but the sermons long, the days of our lives numbered but our worries endless. But in spite of it all, the people of Värmland were no whiners or dullards, were they?

The frost killed the crops all right, the wild animals took their toll among the livestock just as dysentery did among the children, yet people still kept their spirits up, to the very end. Whatever would have happened if they hadn't?

But perhaps this was all possible because every farm had its comforter. One that came to rich and poor alike, that never failed and never tired.

Yet don't imagine that this comforter was anything solemn or splendid, like the word of God or peace of mind or the joy of love! And don't think it was anything base or low, like drinking or gambling. It was simply something quite innocent and ordinary, it was nothing but the fire, burning on the hearth on a winter's night.

My, how cosy and pleasant it made even the smallest cottage! How it went about teasing and joking with the people there, all evening long! It crackled and blazed, almost laughing at them. It spat and hissed, as if it were mocking someone stubborn and angry. Sometimes it was at its wits' end to finish off a gnarled log. It would fill the room with smoke and fumes, as if wanting to let people know it had been given fare too poor to subsist on. Sometimes, just as everyone had found their working pace, it would seize the opportunity to collapse into a pile of cinders so they just had to drop their hands into their laps and laugh out loud until it flared up again. It was usually most mischievous when the mistress of the house brought out her three-legged cauldron to make a meal. Now and then the fire was willing and able, and did its duty quickly and well, but often it danced, lightfooted and dizzy, around the porridge pot for hours without bringing it to a boil.

And how the master's eye gleamed when he came in out of the snow, chilled and soaked through, and was welcomed by the warmth and comfort of the fire! And how good it was to think of the vigilant light pouring out into the dark winter's night as a guide for poor wayfarers or as an omen, a sign of terror to wolverine and wolf!

But the fire could do more than warm and light up and cook meals; it could do something more remarkable than hiss, crackle, spit and smoke. It could revive the love of play in each human soul.

For what is the human soul but a playful flame? It flickers in and above and around us, just as the flames in the fire blaze in and above and around the rough wood. So when those who had gathered around the fire on a winter's night had sat for a while in silence looking into it, the fire began to speak to each and every one of them in its own tongue.

'Kindred soul of mine,' said the flame, 'are you not a flame like me? Why so gloomy and sad?' —

'Kindred flame,' answered the human soul, 'I have been chopping wood and keeping house all day. All I can do is sit staring into you.' —

'I know all that,' said the fire. 'But it's evening now. Do as I do — flicker and flare! Be playful, give warmth!'

And the souls would obey the fire and begin to be playful. They told stories, they guessed riddles, they scraped fiddle strings, they etched roses and vines into their tool handles and tack with. They shared games and melodies, played forfeits and quoted old proverbs. And all the time the icy cold was thawing from their limbs, the peevishness from their spirits. They livened up and began to enjoy themselves. The fire and the games by the fireside gave them the will to go on, however difficult and poverty-stricken their lives were.

One of the main ingredients of these evenings by the fire must have been the stories about great feats and adventures. Everyone, old and young alike, loved to hear stories, and the supply was endless. For, thank heavens, there have always been feats and adventures galore.

Though never have there been so many as in the days of King Charles. He was a hero's hero, and the abundance of stories about him and his men did not perish with him and his reign, but outlived him and were his greatest legacy.

The King was people's favourite hero for stories, but the General from Hedeby, whom people had met and talked to and could describe from head to toe, came a very close second as the subject of their tales.

The General was so strong that he could bend iron as easily as other men bent wicker. Having heard that Mickel, the blacksmith in Svartsjö, made the best horseshoes in those parts, the General rode down to the smithy and asked to have his horse shod. When Mickel brought out a horseshoe, the General asked to have a look at it. The shoe was sturdy and well-made, but the General burst out laughing when he saw it.

'Do you call this iron?' he asked, twisting the horseshoe until it broke. The smith was taken aback at his own poor workmanship.

'That one must have been cracked,' Mickel said, scurrying in to get another. But it met the same fate, though this time the General squeezed it as if it had been a pair of shears, until it split. Then the truth dawned on Mickel.

'You've got to be either King Charles himself or Big Bengt from Hedeby,' he said to the General.

'Good guess, Mickel,' said the General, paying him in full for both four new horseshoes and the two he had broken.

There were lots more stories about the General, and they were told and retold; there was no one in all the district who did not know of him, or respect him and live in awe of him. They also knew of his ring, and that it had been buried with him and then stolen from his grave, human greed being unrestrained.

So it is easy to see that if anything would make people interested and curious and upset, it would be learning that the ring had been recovered and lost again, that Ingilbert had been found dead in the woods, and that the men from Olsby were now behind bars on suspicion of having appropriated the ring. When the churchgoers had made the long walk home on Sunday afternoon, those who had been left behind could hardly wait for them to change their clothes and have a bite to eat before demanding to know everything they had seen and heard, and what kind of sentence people were saying the accused men would get.

People could hardly talk about anything else. Court was in session every evening around the fire in every house and cottage, those of farm folk and gentry alike.

The case was a puzzling, curious one, and hard to come to grips with. It was not easy to reach a unanimous verdict as it was difficult, if not impossible, to believe that the Ivarssons and their foster son would have killed a man for the sake of a ring, however priceless.

First of all, there was Erik Ivarsson. He was a rich man with a great deal of land and property. His only weakness, if it could be considered one, was that he was a proud man, and defensive of his honour at all times. This was what made it so hard to imagine that any gem in the world would lead him to commit a dishonourable act.

His brother, Ivar Ivarsson, was even less open to suspicion. True, he was a poor man, but he had a home with his brother and wanted for nothing. He was so kind-hearted that he had given away all that was his. Why would a man like him contemplate murder and theft?

As for Paul Eliasson, everyone knew he had found great favour with the Ivarssons and was to marry Marit Eriksdotter, who would inherit her father's whole estate. Otherwise, he would have been the likeliest suspect because he was born in Russia, and everyone knew that in Russia theft wasn't considered a sin. Ivar Ivarsson had been a prisoner of war in Russia, and had brought Paul back with him when he was released. Paul had been an orphan of three at the time, and would have died of starvation in his own country. But he had been raised in justice and honesty and had always been a decent man. Marit Eriksdotter and he had grown up as playmates, had loved one another since childhood, and it did not make sense that a man with wealth and happiness in store would hazard it all by stealing a ring.

On the other hand, there was the General to be considered, the General about whom they had heard bedtime stories since they were knee high, the General they knew as they knew their own fathers, the General who was big and strong and trustworthy, the General who was dead and had been robbed of his dearest possession.

The General had known that Ingilbert Bårdsson had the ring with him when he ran off, or he would have let him go in peace and not be killed. The General must also know that the men from Olsby had taken the ring, or they wouldn't have met the Captain on their way down, wouldn't have been arrested, wouldn't have been held in custody.

It was very difficult to come to grips with a case like this, but they trusted the General more than King Charles himself — and most of the trials held in the little cottages returned a verdict of 'guilty.'

It must have come as a great surprise that when the real District Court held session at Broby courthouse and interrogated the accused parties on every point, it found insufficient evidence to convict them. The men refused to plead guilty, and thus the court had to acquit them of the charges of murder and robbery.

However, they were not released, for the verdict of the District Court was subject to examination by the Court of Appeal, and the Court of Appeal was of the opinion that the men from Olsby were guilty and should be hanged.

But not even this sentence was enforced, as the verdict of the Court of Appeals was subject to royal ratification.

And when His Majesty's verdict was published and proclaimed, the people who went to church for once postponed dinner voluntarily until they had expounded it to those who had stayed at home.

To sum it up, the sentence was that since it seemed certain that one of the accused had murdered and robbed, but none of them was willing to admit his guilt, a Divine judgement was to settle the case. At the next court session, in the presence of the judge, the jury and the general public, the accused parties were to play dice. The man who cast the lowest roll would then be considered guilty and be condemned unto death by hanging for his crime, while the other two would immediately be set free to return to their everyday lives.

This was a wise sentence, a just sentence. Everyone here in Värmland was satisfied. Wasn't it good of the old King not to pretend to see more clearly into this obscure case than anyone else, but to appeal to the Almighty in His wisdom? Now the truth of the matter would finally be revealed.

What was more, there was something most unusual about this trial. It was not just one man's word against another's; instead a dead man was party to the case, a dead man demanding the return of his rightful property. There were times when one might hesitate to resort to dice, but this was not one of them. The late General was sure to know who was withholding his possession. And the best part of the royal verdict was that it gave the old General the opportunity to pass judgement.

It was almost as if King Fredrik had wanted to leave the decision to the General. Perhaps he knew, from former days of war, that the General was a trustworthy man. This might be what he had in mind. It wasn't easy to say.

At any rate, of course everyone wanted to be at the courthouse the day the Divine judgement was to be proclaimed. Every single person who was not too old to walk or too little to crawl went along. Nothing as exciting as this had happened for as long as anyone could remember. No one could settle for hearing all about it later, at second hand. No, everyone had to be there.

Since the villages were so few and far between and on ordinary days one could journey for miles and miles without meeting a soul, many people were astonished at the size of the crowd, when the whole district gathered in one place. Row upon row, people had gathered outside the court house. The crowd looked like a swarm of bees hovering around a hive on a summer's day. And it was acting like a swarm of bees, too. The people were in a strange mood, not silent and solemn as at church, not eager and cheerful as at market, but hot-tempered and excitable, obsessed with hatred and vengeance.

And who wouldn't be? They had been weaned on the fear of evil-doers. They had been sung to sleep with lullabies about roving outlaws. They thought of all robbers and murderers as vile, as changelings, as less than human. It never occurred to them that they need show such people any charity.

They knew that some such reprehensible creature was going to be judged that day, and they were glad about it. 'Thank the Lord the world will be one bloodthirsty demon poorer after today,' they thought. 'At least this one will no longer be a threat to us.'

Fortunately, the Divine judgement was not going to be passed in the courtroom, but out of doors. Still the crowd was disappointed to find a company of militiamen surrounding the courthouse yard, making it hard to get up close, and people cast plenty of abuse at the militiamen for standing in the way. They wouldn't ordinarily have done so, but today they were impertinent and pushy.

The people standing nearest the militiamen had had to leave home early to get those places, so they had to stand and wait for hours, and there wasn't much for them to look at while they waited. A bailiff came out and set a large drum in the middle of the yard. That was some consolation, as it assured the crowd that the people inside really meant to hear the case before nightfall. The bailiff also brought out a chair, a table, an inkwell and a pen for the court recorder. At last the bailiff carried out a little cup, in which a pair of dice rattled. He tossed them out onto the drumhead time and again, probably to be sure they weren't weighted and that the rolls were as random as they should be, sometimes falling on one number and sometimes another.

He hurried back in, as was to be expected, since every time he emerged people called out nasty comments and quips at him. They wouldn't have done so ordinarily, but today they weren't capable of common decency.

The militiamen allowed the judge and jurors to pass through the cordon, and they walked or rode up to the courthouse. As each of them appeared the crowd grew lively. There wasn't the whispering and rustling that might ordinarily have been expected. Oh, no. People called out to them and made wisecracks at the top of their lungs. There was no stopping them. Such a large crowd was not easy to control. When the gentry arrived, the militiamen let them through to the courthouse as well. There was Löwensköld from Hedeby and the parson from Bro and the proprietor of the mill from Ekeby and the Captain from Helgesäter and many more, of course. And each one of them got an earful about how lucky he was not to have to stand out here and fight for a place, and plenty more besides.

When the crowd had no one else to hurl abuse at, it aimed its comments at a young woman who was standing as close to the cordon as she possibly could. She was small and slim, and time and again men would try to take away her place, but whenever this happened some people standing nearby shouted that she was the daughter of Erik Ivarsson from Olsby, and when they heard this they let her keep her place in peace.

Instead, they showered her with taunts. She was asked which she would prefer, to see her father or her fiancé hanged. And they commented loudly about the daughter of a thief having the best view.

When people from far off, deep in the forest, wondered how she could have the courage to remain there, they were quickly told. This young lady was no coward. She had been in court each time the case was heard, and not once had she cried, but had remained steadfast throughout. She had nodded and smiled gently at the accused, as if confident they would be set free any day. And seeing her there had renewed their courage. They realized there was at least one person who knew they were innocent. One person who could not conceive that a miserable gold ring could tempt them to commit a crime.

She had sat in the courtroom, beautiful, patient and mild. She had never provoked anyone. Instead, she had gained the sympathy of the judge and jury. Although they would probably not have admitted it, people said that the District Court would never have acquitted the accused men if she had not been there when the case was heard. It was so difficult to believe that anyone Marit Eriksdotter cared for could be a criminal.

And she was here again today, so the prisoners could see her. She was standing here to give them strength and solace. She wanted to pray for them during their trial, and ask God to have mercy on them.

No one could possibly be certain. Although people claim the apple doesn't fall far from the tree, she looked very pure and innocent. And she must have had a loving heart, to be able to go on standing there.

Of course she must have heard every word that was called at her, but she neither answered back nor cried nor tried to flee. She knew the miserable prisoners would be glad to see her, for she was the only one, the only one in the whole crowd, who had taken their plight to heart.

And there was another good thing about her standing there. There were some in the crowd with daughters of their own, as lovely and innocent as she, and their hearts told them they would not have liked to see their daughters in her place.

So the occasional voice was raised in her defense, or at least in protest against the jokers and loudmouths.

It was not only because it meant an end to the long wait, but also for Marit Eriksdotter's sake, that people were relieved to see the courthouse doors open and the procedure commence. In a solemn procession came first the bailiff, the sheriff and the prisoners, who were unbound, neither chained nor handcuffed, although each one was escorted by two militiamen. They were followed by the sexton, the parson, the jurors, the court recorder and the judge. Behind them all came the gentry and a few of the farmers, so highly-respected they had been permitted to cross the cordon.

The sheriff and the prisoners positioned themselves to the left of the courthouse, the judge and jury turned to the right, the gentry stayed in the middle. The court recorder sat at the table with his rolls of paper. The big drum was still in the middle of the yard. Nothing blocked it from view.

From the moment the procession came into sight the crowd grew unruly. A number of big, strong men tried to push their way to the front. They tried especially hard to push Marit Eriksdotter out of the way. But in her terror of not being able to be seen, she bent forward and, small and slim as she was, she crept between the legs of a couple of the militiamen, and passed through the cordon.

This broke all the rules of order, and so the sheriff motioned to the bailiff to get Marit Eriksdotter out of there. The bailiff walked right up to her, put his hand on her shoulder as if to take her into custody, and led her up to the courthouse. But once they had moved into the crowd near the building he let her go. He had seen enough of her to know that if she could just stand near the prisoners she would not try to get away, and if the sheriff wanted a word with her she would be easy to find.

And who had time to think about Marit Eriksdotter now, anyway? The parson and the sexton had stepped forward to the middle of the yard. They removed their hats, and the sexton raised his voice in a hymn. When the people outside the cordon heard the hymn they somehow began to realize that what was about to take place was great and solemn, the most solemn occasion they had ever experienced: an appeal to the Almighty, All-Knowing Lord to speak His will.

The crowd became more and more pious as the parson began to speak. He prayed to Christ, the Son of God, who had once stood before the court of Pontius Pilate, to have mercy on the accused, so that they would not be unjustly sentenced. And he prayed to Him to have mercy on those who were to judge them, so they would not have to condemn an innocent man to death.

And finally, he prayed to Him to have mercy on those assembled there, so they would not have to bear witness to a great injustice as the Jews once did at Golgatha.

They all listened to the parson with their caps in their hands. They left their poor worldly thoughts behind. The mood of the crowd changed. They felt that he had called down God Himself, they felt his presence.

It was a lovely autumn day, with a blue sky, little white clouds, and yellow leaves on all the trees. Flocks of birds kept passing over their heads, flying south. Not often do you see so many migrating birds in one day. They thought this ought to mean something. Should they take it as a sign from God that he approved of their doings?

When the parson had finished, the chief justice stepped forward and read the royal verdict aloud. It was long, with many turns of phrase that made it difficult to follow. But they could understand that the secular powers were somehow laying down their sword and sceptre, their wisdom and knowledge, and appealing to the counsel of the Lord. And they prayed, each man prayed, that He would bring them help and guidance.

Then the sheriff picked up the dice and requested that the judge and several others roll them to check that they were all right. And, with a singular trembling, the crowd heard the sound of the dice falling on the drumhead. These tiny objects that had been the undoing of so many men, were they now to be seen as worthy of interpreting the will of God?

When the dice had been tested, the three prisoners were brought forward. The cup was first given to Erik Ivarsson, who was the eldest. As he handed it to him, the sheriff explained that this was not yet the deciding roll. This one was just to determine who would be first.

The result of this first round was that Paul Eliasson rolled lowest and Ivar Ivarsson highest. And so he was to be first.

The three accused men had on the same clothes as when they met the Captain on their way down from the summer pasture, but now they were torn and filthy. The clothes seemed to reflect the ragged and worn state of the men wearing them. But it looked to all as if Ivar Ivarsson had held up the best of the three. This was probably because he had been a soldier and was inured to suffering from war and captivity. He still stood up tall, and looked dauntless and brave.

When Ivar Ivarsson stepped up to the drum and took the cup containing the dice, the sheriff tried to instruct him as to how to hold it and how to roll. At this, the old man's face took on a smile.

'This isn't the first time I've chanced a little roll, sheriff,' he said in a voice audible to all. 'I've passed many an evening out there on the steppe playing craps with Big Bengt from Hedeby . But I never expected to find myself playing against him again.'

The sheriff tried to hurry him, but the crowd liked listening to him speak. It took a brave man to joke at such a critical moment.

He clasped the cup with both hands, and the crowd could see he was praying. After saying the Lord's Prayer, he shouted: 'And now, Sweet Jesus, who knows of my innocence, I pray that in Your mercy You will give me a low roll, as I have neither children nor sweetheart to weep over me.'

Having said this, he cast the dice so hard against the drumhead that it resounded.

Everyone standing outside wished at that moment to see Ivar Ivarsson go free. They liked him because he was fearless and good. They couldn't understand how they could ever have thought him a criminal.

It was nigh-on intolerable to stand so far away and not know how the dice had fallen. The judge and the sheriff bent forward to see, the jurors and the gentry approached and saw the cast. Everyone looked surprised; one or two nodded to Ivar Ivarsson, a few shook his hand, but the crowd was told nothing. A grumbling and grousing began.

At that the judge signalled to the sheriff, who climbed the steps to the courthouse to make himself seen and heard.

'Ivar Ivarsson has rolled two sixes, the highest possible roll.'

People realized that Ivar Ivarsson had been acquitted, and were pleased. Quite a few even shouted:

'Good luck to you, Ivar Ivarsson!'

But what happened next filled everyone with amazement. Paul Eliasson burst into shouts of joy, tore his cap from his head and tossed it in the air. This came so unexpectedly that the guards could not stop him. People could not help but wonder over Paul Eliasson. Although Ivar Ivarsson had been like a father to him, his own life was now at stake. Could he really delight so in seeing one of the others acquitted?

Order was soon restored. The authorities returned to the right, the prisoners and their guards to the left; other spectators moved over to the courthouse, leaving the drum free in the middle, fully visible from all sides. It was now Erik Ivarsson's turn to look life or death in the face.

A broken old man stepped forth, stumbling and hesitant. People seemed hardly to recognize him. Could this be Erik

Ivarsson, who had always appeared strong and authoritative? His eyes were glazed, and many people thought he could hardly be fully conscious of his actions. But once he had the cup containing the dice in his hand, he attempted to straighten up and say a few words.

'I thank God my brother Ivar is now a free man,' he said, 'for although I stand here as innocent as he, he has always been the better man. And I pray to Christ our Lord that He let me roll a bad roll, so my daughter may marry the man she loves, and live happily with him until the end of her days.'

As is true of many old men, all Erik Ivarsson's past strength now seemed to be gathered in his voice. His words were heard by all, and the crowd was deeply moved. It was quite unlike Erik Ivarsson to admit that anyone was his better, and to hope for his own death to ensure the happiness of another. There was not a soul in all the crowd who could go on thinking of him as a robber and a thief. People stood there with tears in their eyes, praying to God to give him a high roll.

He barely shook the dice, but just emptied the cup and let them fall. His eyes were too weak to count up the dice; he didn't even look down, but just stood staring into space.

The judge and the others hurried forward. And the crowd saw the same surprised expressions on their faces as at the previous roll.

It was as if the crowd outside the cordon realized what had happened long before the sheriff announced the result.

One woman cried: 'God bless you, Erik Ivarsson!' and then the crowd could be heard shouting: 'Praised be the Lord for helping you, Erik Ivarsson!'

· Paul Eliasson's cap flew into the air like the time before, and the crowd began to wonder once more. Wasn't he aware of what this meant for him?

Erik Ivarsson stood there, dull and indifferent, no relief visible on his face. People thought he must be waiting for the sheriff to announce the roll, but even when this was done and he heard that he had rolled two sixes like his brother, he remained listless. He wanted to totter back to his former place, but he was so exhausted that the bailiff had to put his arm around him to hold him upright.

Now it was Paul Eliasson's turn to step up to the drum and try his luck, and the eyes of the crowd turned upon him. Long before this trial, it had been the general opinion that he must be the real criminal. And now he was already doomed, so to speak, since there was no way his roll could be higher than the Ivarsson brothers'.

This idea didn't seem to bother anyone until they noticed that Marit Eriksdotter had crept close up to Paul Eliasson.

He did not embrace her, they exchanged no kiss or hug. She just stood pressed close, close beside him, and he put his arm around her waist. No one could actually say how long they had been standing that way, for everyone's attention had been fixed on the drum.

At any rate, there they stood, joined somehow despite the guards and the intimidating authorities, despite the thousands of spectators, despite the terrible game in which they were involved, where the stakes were life or death.

It was love, and of a sort beyond all worldly love, that united them. They might have been standing like this on the path across the meadows one summer morning, after having danced all night and spoken, for the first time, of becoming man and wife. They might have been standing like this after their first communion, feeling their souls purified of all sin. They might have been standing like this if they had both been through the horrors of death, reached the other shore and been reunited, to find that they belonged together for all eternity.

She stood looking at him with pure love, and there was something about them that told people Paul Eliasson was the very man they should pity. He was a growing tree that would not be allowed to blossom and bear fruit, he was a rye field that would be trampled before yielding any of its richess.

He let his arm fall from Marit's waist and followed the sheriff to the drum. He did not look worried as he held the cup. Nor did he speak to the people, but turned to Marit.

'Never fear!' he said. 'God knows, I am as innocent as the others.'

After which he shook the dice playfully and let them roll around in the cup until they came up over the edge and fell onto the drumhead.

He stood motionless, following them with his gaze, but when at last they both had stopped, the crowd did not have to wait for the sheriff to announce the roll. Paul Eliasson cried out in his own loud voice:

'I've rolled two sixes, Marit. I've rolled two sixes, just like the others.'

It never occurred to him that this could mean anything but an acquittal, and he was too excited to stand still. He leapt, tossed his cap in the air, hugged and kissed the guard who was beside him.

And everyone thought: 'You can see he's Russian. If he'd been Swedish he wouldn't have been so quick to rejoice.'

The judge, the sheriff, the jury and gentry walked up to the drum, slowly and calmly, and examined the dice. But they did not look pleased this time. They shook their heads, and none of them congratulated Paul Eliasson on his roll.

The sheriff went over to the courthouse steps for the third time and announced: 'Paul Eliasson has rolled two sixes, the highest possible cast.'

There was a tumult in the crowd, but no rejoicing. Although it did not occur to anyone that they had been deceived — such things just did not happen — everyone was upset because Divine Judgement had not clarified the case.

Were all three of the accused men equally innocent, or were

they all equally guilty?

They saw Captain Löwensköld scurry over to the judge. He must have wanted to say that nothing was settled, but the judge quite abruptly turned his back on him.

The judge and the jury went along into the courthouse to consider the matter, and while they were gone no one dared move or speak, hardly even whisper. Even Paul Eliasson stayed still. It seemed to have struck him that Divine Judgement was open to more than one interpretation.

The Court resumed after brief deliberation, and the judge announced that the District Court was inclined to interpret the result to mean that all three of the accused should be acquitted.

Paul Eliasson tore himself away from his guards and tossed his cap in the air once more in great rejoicing, but this was a hair's breadth early, for the judge went on:

'But the opinion of this District Court is to be submitted to His Majesty by a courier, who will be sent to Stockholm this very day, the accused to be retained in custody until the royal ratification of the verdict of the District Court has been received.'

VIII

One autumn day thirty years or so after that remarkable game of dice at Broby courthouse, Marit Eriksdotter was sitting on the steps in front of the little cabin she lived in on the big farm at Olsby, knitting a pair of baby's mittens. She wanted to knit a pretty pattern into them, with checks and stripes, so the baby she was making them for would like them, but she couldn't call a pattern to mind.

After sitting for a long time sketching on the step with one of her knitting needles, she went into the cabin and opened her chest to find a knitted pattern she could copy. Way down at the bottom she found a cap, artfully designed in different colours and patterns, and after a moment's hesitation, she took it along out to the steps.

Examining the cap from both sides to figure out the pattern, Marit noticed that the moths had been at it. 'Well, goodness knows why they shouldn't have,' she thought. 'It must be at least thirty years since anyone wore it. How lucky I happened to find it in my chest, before it got any worse.'

The moths seemed to have taken the greatest pleasure in the big, colourful tassel, because when Marit began to shake the cap out, pieces of yarn from it flew every which way. The tassel fell off, dropping into her lap, and picking it up to see if it was too far gone to repair, she saw a glitter inside. Eagerly separating the strands of yarn, she found a large gold signet ring, set with a red jewel, sewn into the tassel with coarse linen thread.

The tassel and the cap dropped from her hands. She had never seen the ring before, but there was no need for her to look for the royal insignia on the jewel or to read the words etched inside the band to know what ring it was and to whom it belonged. Leaning against the railing, pale and still as death, she shut her eyes. Her heart felt as if it would break.

This was the ring for which her father, Erik Ivarsson, her uncle, Ivar Ivarsson, and her fiance, Paul Eliasson, had given their lives, only for her to find it now, sewn into the tassel of Paul's cap!

How did it get there? When did it get there? Had Paul known it was there?

No! She said to herself at once that he could not possibly have known.

She remembered how he had waved that very cap and tossed it high into the air when he thought that both he and the old Ivarsson brothers were acquitted.

She saw it all, as if it had been yesterday. The mob, first resentful and vengeful toward her and her nearest and dearest but convinced, in the end, of their innocence. She remembered the lovely, deep blue autumn sky, the flocks of migrating birds flying aimlessly over the courthouse yard. Paul had noticed them, too, and at that very moment, as she stood leaning against him, he had whispered to her that his soul would soon be roving around on high, aimless as a little bird. And he had asked her if he might come and live under the eaves at Olsby.

No, Paul could not have known that there were stolen goods concealed in the cap he tossed up into the beautiful autumn sky.

There had been another day as well. Her heart shrank every time she thought of it, as she was forced to now. An edict had arrived from Stockholm stating that the Divine verdict was to be interpreted to mean that the accused were all equally guilty and were to be hanged by the neck until dead.

She had been present when the sentence was enacted, so that the men she loved would know that there was one person who believed in them and grieved for them. But she need hardly have been witness to the hanging for that reason alone. People had changed their minds since the day of the trial. Every member of the crowd outside the cordon was kind to her. After due consideration and much discussion, the people had determined that the Divine judgement ought to have been interpreted to mean that all three of the accused men were equally innocent. The old General had let them all cast the highest possible roll. It could mean nothing else. None of them had taken his ring.

A general lamentation arose when the three men were led out. Women had wept, the men had stood there with clenched fists and resolute faces. People claimed that, like Jerusalem, Bro parish was sure to come to ruin for taking the lives of innocent men. People had called comforting words to the condemned men and hooted at the hangmen. And many were the curses called down upon the head of Captain Löwensköld. People claimed he had travelled to Stockholm, and it was his fault the interpretation of the Divine judgement had gone against the accused men.

At any rate, this feeling that everyone had shared her faith and trust was what had helped her through that day. And not just that day, but all the time since. If the people around her had thought of her as the daughter of a murderer, she would not have been able to face living.

Paul Eliasson had been the first to mount the little wooden platform under the gallows. After kneeling down to pray, he had turned toward the parson standing beside him and made a request. After this Marit had seen the parson remove the cap from his head. When it was all over, the parson had given the cap to Marit, with love from Paul. He had sent it to her as a sign, that he had been thinking of her at the very end.

Could she ever imagine that Paul would have sent her the cap to remember him by if he had known it concealed the stolen goods? No, if one thing was certain in this world, it was this: he had not known that the ring, once worn on a dead man's finger, was hidden in the cap.

Marit Eriksdotter bent hastily forward, held up the cap and examined it. 'Where can Paul have got this cap from?' she wondered. 'Neither I nor anyone else on the farm knitted it for him. He must have bought it at market, or maybe he swapped with someone for it.'

She turned the cap around once more, examining the pattern. 'This must have been a nice bright cap to see,' she thought. 'Paul loved colourful things. He was never satisfied with the grey clothes we wove him, but wanted some colour in his homespun. He like red caps best, with big tassels. I'm sure he loved this one.' —

She set the cap down and leaned back against the railing once more, to look into the past.

She was in the forest that morning, when Ingilbert had been frightened to death. She saw how Paul and her father and uncle had stood bent over his corpse. The two old men had decided that they should carry Ingilbert back to the village and gone to chop branches for the litter. But Paul had hung back for a moment to look at Ingilbert's cap. The bright patterns knitted in red, blue and white made him want it for his own, and when no one was looking he had simply traded. He had meant no harm. Perhaps he had only thought to keep it for a little while. The cap he gave Ingilbert in return was undoubtedly just as good, but less colourful, less artistic.

Ingilbert, however, had sewn the ring into his cap before leaving home. Perhaps he had expected to be pursued and had wanted to hide it. And when he fell, no one thought of looking in his cap for the ring. Least of all Paul Eliasson.

That was how it had happened! She would have sworn to it, but you never know for certain.

She put the ring back into the chest and, cap in hand, went out to the cow shed to speak to the dairymaid.

'Come out into the daylight, Märta,' she said, 'and help me with a pattern I can't make out.'

When the dairymaid appeared, she held out the cap to her.

'I know you've done a lot of knitting, Märta,' she said. 'I want to knit this pattern, but I can't figure it out. Could you have a look at it? You know more about this sort of thing than I do.'

The dairymaid took the cap and glanced at it. She looked surprised. She moved out of the shadow of the cow shed and examined it anew.

'Where did you find this?' she asked.

'It's been in my chest for years,' said Marit. 'Why do you ask?'

'Because I knitted this cap for my brother Ingilbert the summer before his death,' said the dairymaid. 'I never saw it again after the morning he left home. How did it get here?'

'He may have lost it when he fell down,' said Marit. 'Maybe one of our farmhands found it in the woods and brought it home. — But if it awakens bitter memories for you, perhaps you would rather not copy the pattern for me?'

'If I may borrow it, you'll have the pattern tomorrow,' said the dairymaid.

She took the cap back into the cow shed with her, but Marit could hear the tears in her voice.

'No, you mustn't do it if it causes you pain,' she said.

'You know I would do anything for you, Marit.'

It had actually been Marit who had realized that Märta Bårdsdotter was left alone up in the forest after the death of her father and brother, and who had offered to make her dairymaid on the big farm at Olsby. Märta never forgot to show her gratitude for having been given the opportunity to come back down and live among others.

Marit returned to the cabin steps and picked up her knitting, but could not settle down to it, so she rested her head against the railing as before and tried to figure out what her next step should be.

If anyone on the farm at Olsby had known what women look like who have relinquished worldly life to join a convent, he would have said that Marit looked like such a woman. Her face was pale, parched and absolutely unlined. A stranger would probably have found it impossible to say whether she was young or old. There was something peaceful and calm about her, as there is about those who have ceased having desires of their own. Although she never looked truly happy, neither did she ever look overcome by sorrow.

After the terrible blow, Marit had felt that her life was finished in every way. She had inherited the big farm after her father's death, but had soon realized that if she wished to keep it she would have to marry, to give the farm a master. In order to be spared this, she had turned the whole farm over to one of her nephews on the sole condition that she should be lodged and boarded there for as long as she lived.

She was content with this and had no second thoughts. There was no danger of her feeling idle. People had come to trust in her wisdom and kindness, and whenever anyone fell ill, Marit was sent for. She also had the confidence of the children, and her little house was usually full of youngsters. They knew she always had time to help them with their little worries.

Now as Marit sat thinking about what she should do with the ring, a great fury rose inside her. She realized how easily it might have been discovered. Why hadn't the General seen to it that it was found? He had known where it was all along, she could see that now But why had he not made them examine Ingilbert's cap? Instead he had let three innocent men go to their deaths because of the ring. He had been powerful enough to do that, but not to make the ring come to light.

Marit's first thought had been to take her tale to the parson and turn the ring over to him, but no, she didn't want to do that.

Because wherever Marit went, to church or to someone's home, she met with great esteem. She had never experienced the disdain usually felt by the daughter of a criminal. People held the firm conviction that some wrong had been done, and they wanted to make it up to her. Even the gentry would be sure to say a few words to her if they saw her outside church. And members of the family from Hedeby, too — not the Captain himself, but his wife and daughter-in-law — had occasionally tried to approach Marit. But she had always turned her back on them. She hadn't said a word to anyone from the manor since the trial.

Was she now supposed to step forward and admit that, in a way, the people from Hedeby had been right? The ring had turned out to be in the possession of the men from Olsby after all. People might even say that the men had known where it was all along, and had endured imprisonment and interrogation in the hope of being able to sell it after their release.

At any rate Marit realized that it would seem a vindication of the Captain, and even of his father, if she handed over the ring and revealed where she had found it. And Marit did not want to do anything that was beneficial or advantageous to the Löwen-skölds.

Captain Löwensköld was now a gentleman of eighty, rich and

powerful, honoured and respected. The King had made him a Baron, and he had never suffered the least misfortune. His sons were fine men, and they, too, were wealthy and had married well.

That man had robbed Marit of everything, absolutely everything. There she was, all alone, with no property, no husband, no children, and it was all his fault. She had waited for years for some punishment to strike him, but none had come.

Marit shot up out of these deep thoughts, brought back to the present by the patter of feet across the yard. She realized they were heading her way.

It was two boys of about ten or eleven. One of them was the farmer's son, Nils, the other she didn't know. Just as she had expected, they had come to ask her a favour.

'Marit,' said Nils, 'this is Adrian from Hedeby. We were over there rolling our hoops along the road when we got into a fight and I tore Adrian's cap.'

Marit sat staring at Adrian. A lovely child, he looked gentle and kind. Her hand went to her heart. Seeing a Löwensköld always caused her anguish and pain.

'We've made it up now,' said Nils, ' and I wondered if you would be willing to mend Adrian's cap before he goes home.'

'Yes,' said Marit. 'I'll do it.'

She took the torn cap and rose to go into the cabin.

'It must be a sign from God,' she mumbled to herself. To the boys she said:

'You two play out here for a few minutes. This won't take long.'

She shut the cabin door behind her and made certain she was left alone while she darned the holes in Adrian Löwensköld's knitted cap.

IX

A few more years passed without the ring being heard of at all. But, in 1788 Miss Malvina Spaak happened to become housekeeper at Hedeby. She was from a poor clergyman's family in Sörmland, had never before set foot in the province of Värmland, and hadn't the slightest notion of the state of affairs at the manor where she was to serve.

The very day she arrived, however, she was called in to see Baroness Löwensköld, who confided something most peculiar to her.

'I think it only right,' said the mistress of the house, 'for you to be told at once, Miss Spaak, that Hedeby is undeniably a haunted house. Not infrequently, on the stairs or in the halls, and sometimes even in the rooms, we encounter a big, heavy-set man, dressed in cavalry boots and a blue military coat, rather like one of the old Carolines. Suddenly he is right there in front of you, when you open a door or reach a landing, and before you can even

73

wonder who he might be he is gone. He has never done any harm. In fact, I think he only means well, and I hope you will not be frightened when you meet him.'

Miss Spaak was twenty-one at the time, slim and agile, extraordinarily capable when it came to every kind of chore and task, enterprising and resolute, and wherever she put a hand in the household ran like clockwork. But she was extremely frightened of ghosts, and she would never have taken the situation at Hedeby if she had known of the haunting in advance. But now she was here, and a poor girl must really think twice before she gives up a good place. So she curtsied to the Baroness, thanked her for the warning, and assured her that she had no intention of letting herself be frightened.

'We really haven't the slightest idea, Miss Spaak, of why he haunts this place,' her mistress continued. 'My daughters think he quite resembles my husband's paternal grandfather, General Löwensköld, the man in that portrait over there, and so they call him the Gen'ral. But I am sure you understand that no one actually thinks the spirit of the General himself — who is said to have been a man of the highest repute — is actually walking. In truth it's an absolute mystery to us. And if you hear any explanations coming from the servants, I hope you will have the sense to pay no attention.'

Miss Spaak curtsied once more, and assured her mistress that she never gave the servants the slightest opportunity to gossip about the gentry. With this, her audience was concluded.

Although Miss Spaak was nothing but a poor housekeeper, she came from a good family and was therefore allowed to eat at table with the Baron's family, as were the manager of the estate and the children's tutor. What was more she was lithe and comely, small and slim, fair-haired and rosy-cheeked, and so pleasing to the eye that she was not unbecoming to the dinner table of the gentry. Everyone found her to be a kind-hearted soul, always able to make herself useful, and she was well-liked from the very start.

She was quick to note that the ghost-walking the Baroness had described to her was a common subject of conversation at mealtimes. Sometimes one of the young mistresses, sometimes the tutor would say: 'I'm the one who's seen the Gen'ral today,' as if this were something to set store by and boast of.

Not a day passed without someone asking her if she had not yet met the ghost, and each time she had to admit that she had not, she began to sense that she fell in their esteem. It seemed to make her inferior to the manager and the tutor, who had each seen the ghost on numerous occasions.

Actually, Miss Spaak had never encountered people with such an offhand attitude toward a ghost, and she suspected from the start that something dreadful would come of it. She said to herself that if there really was a being from the 'other side' in the house, he must be an unfortunate soul who needed help from the living to find peace in his grave. She was a resolute person, and if it had been up to her the matter would have been looked into more seriously and got to the bottom of, instead of providing a topic for dinner conversation.

But Miss Spaak knew what her position demanded, and not a word of criticism of the family's behaviour ever crossed her lips. She was careful never to take part in the joking about the spirit, and she kept her apprehensions to herself.

Miss Spaak had been at Hedeby a whole month before she got to see the ghost. But one morning when she had been in the attic counting out some washing, she unexpectedly found herself face to face on the stairs with a man who quickly stepped aside to let her pass. It was broad daylight, and the thought never crossed her mind that he might be a ghost. She simply wondered what business a stranger could have in the attic, and turned around to ask him what he was doing there. But there was not a soul to be seen on the stairs. Miss Spaak went back up into the attic, searching every dark nook and cranny in the expectation of catching a thief red-handed. But when she found no human being there, she suddenly realized what was going on.

'What a fool I am!' she burst out. 'That was naturally none other than the Gen'ral.'

But of course, but of course! The fellow had been wearing a blue coat just like the old General in the portrait, and the same kind of huge cavalry boots. She had not recognized his face exactly, his features had been somewhat grey and hazy.

Miss Spaak stayed up in the attic for some time, gathering her wits. Her teeth were chattering and her knees were weak. If there had not been dinner to see to she would never have been able to get back down the stairs. At once she determined to keep what she had seen to herself and not let the others joke with her about it.

But she couldn't get the Gen'ral off her mind, and she must have had a strange expression on her face, for almost as soon as they sat down to dinner the master's son, a young man of nineteen who had just come home from the university at Uppsala for Christmas, turned toward her.

'Miss Spaak has seen the Gen'ral today,' he said, and this brusque announcement was too much for her to deny.

At once Miss Spaak found herself the centre of attention. Everyone at the table asked her questions, which she answered as briefly as possible. Unfortunately she could not deny that she had been a bit frightened, which the others found incredibly funny. Scared of the Gen'ral! It would never have occurred to them.

Miss Spaak had long ago noted that the Baron and Baroness never took part in joking about the Gen'ral. They just let the others carry on uninterrupted. Now she observed that this young scholar took the matter far more seriously than the other young people.

'Personally,' he said, 'I envy anyone who gets to see the Gen'ral. I would like to help him, but he has never made himself visible to me.'

He said this with genuine desire and with such a lovely look in his eyes that Miss Spaak lodged a silent prayer that his wish might soon come true. The young Baron would be sure to have mercy on the poor spirit and return him to the peace of his grave.

In the days that followed Miss Spaak seemed to be more the object of the spirit's attention than anyone else. She saw him so often that she almost grew accustomed to him. He made sudden, rapid appearances, sometimes on the stairs, sometimes in a vestibule, sometimes in a dark corner of the kitchen.

Never could the slightest reason for his appearance be found. Miss Spaak had a vague suspicion there was something in the house the spirit was looking for. But as he vanished the very second any human being set eye on him, she could not possibly determine his intent.

Contrary to what the Baroness had said, it seemed to Miss Spaak that all the young people at Hedeby were completely convinced that it was the ghost of old General Löwensköld who walked.

'He doesn't like being in the grave,' the young mistresses would say, 'and he's interested in seeing what we're up to here at Hedeby. Who could hold that simple pleasure against him?'

Miss Spaak, who had to lock herself into the larder so her teeth could chatter out of earshot of the mocking scullery maids every time she saw the Gen'ral, would undoubtedly have preferred him to show less interest in the goings on at Hedeby. But she realized that the rest of the family would actually have missed him.

For example, there were the long evenings by the fire. People sat spinning or embroidering, and sometimes there was nothing left to read or talk about. Suddenly one of the young mistresses would raise a shout. She had seen a face, no, she had really just seen two rows of gleaming teeth, against the window pane. Everyone scurried to light a lantern, open the door and rush out, the

Baroness in the lead and all the other women close behind, to see who was disturbing the peace. But of course there was nothing to be seen. They all went back in, closed the shutters, shrugged their shoulders and said that it had probably just been the Gen'ral. But in the meanwhile they had perked up. Now that they had something to think about, the spinning wheels picked up speed, the conversation resumed.

The entire family was convinced that as soon as they vacated the dining room in the evenings, the Gen'ral took up residence there, and that if they had dared to enter the room they would have found him in it. They had nothing against his being there. Miss Spaak thought it pleased them to think their restless forefather had a nice warm room to be in.

One of the Gen'ral's peculiarities was that he expected to find the room neat and tidy when he moved in. Each evening the housekeeper would see the Baroness and the young mistresses fold up their needlework and take it out with them. Even the spinning wheels and the embroidery frames were moved to another room. Not so much as a loose thread was left on the floor.

Miss Spaak, whose sleeping quarters were next to the dining room, awoke one night at the sound of an object hitting the other side of the wall by her bed with a thud, and then rolling along the floor. She had hardly gathered her wits when there was another slam and she heard the rolling sound again; then all of this happened twice more.

'What in the world's he doing in there now?' she sighed, knowing who must be causing the commotion. He was really not a nice kind of neighbour to have. She lay cold and shivering all night in fear that the Gen'ral was going to come and squeeze the life out of her.

She made both the scullery maid and the housemaid accompany her the next morning when she went into the dining room to see what had happened. But nothing was broken, no disorder could be seen, except for four apples in the middle of the floor. Oh me, oh my. They had been eating apples by the fire the evening before and had left four on the mantlepiece. But this had displeased the Gen'ral. Miss Spaak had to pay the price of a sleepless night for her negligence.

On the other hand, Miss Spaak could never forget that she once received real proof of the Gen'ral's affection.

There had been a party at Hedeby, with a big dinner and a lots of company. Miss Spaak had her hands full, with roasts on all the spits, pastries and patés in the oven and soup kettles and saucepans over the fire on the hearth. And this was not all. Miss Spaak also had to be in the dining room to oversee the table setting, take charge of the silver as the Baroness herself counted it out for her, remember to have the wine and beer brought up from the cellar and the candles set straight in the chandeliers. And bearing in mind that the kitchen at Hedeby was in a separate wing, which meant that you had to run across the yard to get there, and that the whole place was full of company, not to mention unfamiliar servants, it's not hard to see that this undertaking required the leadership of a skilful person.

But everything went smoothly and according to plan. There were no fingerprints on the glasses, no foul-tasting lumps in the paté, the beer was foamy, the consomme well-seasoned and the coffee just the right strength. Miss Spaak had proven herself, and the Baroness had complimented her personally, saying that things couldn't have been better.

Until the awful setback occurred, that is. When the house-keeper was going to return the silver to the Baroness two spoons were missing, one soup spoon and one teaspoon.

It caused a great stir. In those days this was the worst thing that could happen in a household, for some of the silver to be missing. Hedeby became feverish, desperate. People did nothing but search. They recalled that a gypsy had been in the kitchen on the very day of the party, and some people were prepared to go deep into the woods to look for her. Everyone was suspicious and unreasonable. The mistress of the house suspected the housekeeper, the housekeeper suspected the scullery maids who suspected one another and all the world. At one time or another each one appeared red-eyed from crying her eyes out in fear that someone else thought she had appropriated the two spoons.

This had gone on for a couple of days, nothing had been found, and Miss Spaak was at her wits' end. She had been in the pigsty and searched the troughs to see if the spoons might be there. She had made her way up to the maids' part of the attic and stealthily gone through their little clothing chests. All this had been in vain, and now she could not think where else to look. It was clear to her that the Baroness and the whole household suspected her, the stranger. She would be given notice, she was sure, if she did not resign first.

Miss Spaak was weeping over the cooker, her tears sizzling on the hot stove top, when she had the feeling she ought to turn around. She did so and, lo and behold, there was the Gen'ral over by the kitchen wall, pointing to a shelf that was so high and difficult to reach that no one ever thought of putting anything there.

The Gen'ral vanished as usual the very second he was seen, but Miss Spaak went over to where he had been pointing. She took the stepladder from the larder, stood it by the shelf, stretched up her hand and found a dirty old dishtowel. But rolled up in the towel were both silver spoons.

How did they get there? It must have happened completely by chance. In the hustle and bustle of preparing a big party, anything could happen. The dishtowel had been cast aside, had been in someone's way, and the silver spoons had gone with it, unobserved.

Anyway, there they were and, beaming, Miss Spaak carried them in to the Baroness and was reinstated as everyone's right-hand woman and favourite assistant.

It's an ill wind that blows no good. Later that spring when young Baron Adrian came home and heard that the Gen'ral had shown Miss Spaak an unusual courtesy, he at once began to pay special attention to her. As often as he could, he sought her out in the drawing room or in the kitchen. Sometimes his excuse was that he needed some new line for his fishing rod, sometimes he said it was the wonderful smell of fresh Lenten buns that had drawn him in. On these occasions he always turned the conversation to the supernatural. He encouraged the housekeeper to talk about the hauntings on the big estates in Sörmland, such as Julita and Eriksberg, and asked her what she thought of them.

But mostly he wanted to talk about the Gen'ral. He said he couldn't discuss the matter with the others because they only saw the funny side of it. Personally he felt compassion for the poor ghost and wanted to help him to find peace. He only wished he knew how to do it!

Miss Spaak then said that in her humble opinion there was something in the house for which he was searching.

The young Baron paled slightly. He gave the housekeeper a searching look.

'Ma foi, Miss Spaak, what an idea! But I assure you that if anyone here at Hedeby had anything the Gen'ral wanted, we wouldn't hesitate to return it to him. Not for a moment, Miss Spaak.'

Miss Spaak knew full well that the young Baron sought her out to talk about the ghost and for no other reason whatsoever, but he was such a charming young man, and so handsome. In fact, if you asked her, he was more than handsome. He carried himself with his head slightly bowed; there was something pensive about him, and believe it or not some people even thought he was altogether too sombre. But this was only because they didn't know him. Sometimes he would toss his head, make jokes and be more mischievous than anyone else. But no matter what he was doing, his movements, his voice and his smile were all indescribably pleasing.

One summer Sunday Miss Spaak had been to church and was walking homeward, following a little path that cut diagonally across the fields belonging to the parsonage. A few other members of the congregation had turned off the same way, and since Miss Spaak was in a hurry, she had to pass a woman whose pace was far too slow for her. A moment later she came to a rather awkward stile and, being the helpful person she was, Miss Spaak remembered passing the slower walker, and waited to help her over. When she extended her hand, Miss Spaak noticed that the woman was not as old as she had appeared at first. Her skin was remarkably smooth and pale, and Miss Spaak thought she might actually not be more than fifty. Although she was clearly no more than a common farm woman she had a singular sort of dignity, as if she had experienced something that had raised her above her station.

After Miss Spaak assisted the woman over the stile, the two of them walked side by side along the narrow path.

'I suppose you are the one who keeps house at Hedeby, Miss?' said the woman.

'Yes, I am,' answered Miss Spaak.

'I was just wondering how you like it there.'

'Why wouldn't anyone like working at such a good place?' Miss Spaak asked guardedly.

'Well, people do say the house is haunted.'

'But you should never believe people's talk,' Miss Spaak reprimanded her gently.

'No, no you certainly shouldn't, I know that's true,' said the woman.

There was silence for some time. It was clear that the woman knew more than she was letting on, and Miss Spaak was actually dying to ask her all kinds of questions. But it wouldn't be right or fitting.

It was the woman who reopened the conversation.

'I like the looks of you, Miss,' she said, ' and so I want to give you a piece of advice. Don't stay too long at Hedeby, because the man who walks there is not easy to deal with. He won't give up until he gets what he wants.'

Miss Spaak had at first intended to thank the old woman for the warning, a bit superciliously. But these last words provoked her curiosity.

'What does he want? Do you know what it is?'

'Haven't you been told, Miss?' said the old woman. 'Well, I'll say no more then. It may be best to know nothing of it.'

With these words she shook Miss Spaak's hand, turned off onto another path, and was soon out of sight.

Miss Spaak was extremely careful not to speak of this conversation to the whole family at dinner, but later in the day when Baron Adrian had sought her out in the dairy, she revealed to him what the strange woman had said. He was extremely surprised indeed.

'That must have been Marit Eriksdotter from Olsby,' he said. 'I'll have you know, Miss Spaak, that was the first time in thirty years she has said a kind word to anyone from Hedeby. Once she mended a cap of mine one of the Olsby boys had torn, but she looked as if she would rather have scratched my eyes out.'

'But does she know what it is the General is searching for?'

'She knows better than anyone, Miss Spaak. And I know too. My father has told me the whole story. But my parents don't want my sisters to hear it. It would make them afraid of ghosts, and then we might not be able to go on living here. And I have also been prohibited from telling you.'

'God forbid!' said Miss Spaak. 'If the Baron has prohibited it . . .'

'It hurts me,' said Baron Adrian, 'because I think, Miss, that you could help me.'

'Ah, if only I could!'

'For, I repeat,' said Baron Adrian, 'I wish to help the poor ghost find peace. I am not afraid of him. I shall follow him the moment he calls for me. Why does he appear to everyone but me?'

X

Adrian Löwensköld lay sleeping in a gable bedroom in the attic when he was awakened by a slight noise. He opened his eyes, and as the shutters were not latched and it was a light summer night, he clearly saw the door glide open. He thought the draught had done it until he saw a dark shape fill the opening and lean forward, gazing intently into the room.

Adrian could quite distinctly see an old man, dressed in an outdated cavalry uniform. An elk skin jerkin protruded from his coat, which was open at the throat, his boots went up over the knee, and his long sabre was raised, as if to keep it from rattling.

'I do believe this is the Gen'ral,' the young Baron thought. 'Very well. I'll show him someone who's not afraid of him.'

Everyone else who had seen the Gen'ral said that he vanished as soon as they set eyes on him. But not this time. The Gen'ral stayed in the doorway long after Adrian discovered his presence. In a few moments, when he appeared to feel confident that Adrian would go on looking at him, he raised a hand and beckoned to him.

Adrian sat straight up in bed. 'It's now or never,' he thought. 'He is finally appealing for my help, and I shall follow him'.

Actually, he had been anticipating this moment for many years. He had been bracing himself for it, focusing his strength to meet it. He had always known it was something he would have to face.

He did not want to keep the Gen'ral waiting, so he got straight out of bed, just grabbing a sheet to wrap around himself.

Not until he was in the middle of the room did it occur to him that it might in fact be a risky matter to place oneself in the hands of a being from the spirit world, and he shrank back. But then he saw the Gen'ral stretch out both arms beseechingly toward him.

'What kind of nonsense is this?' he asked himself. 'Am I frightened before I've so much as left the room?'

He approached the door. The General slipped before him into the attic, moving backwards all the time, as if to remain assured that the young man was following him.

When Adrian was about to cross the threshold of his room and go out into the attic, he felt another shiver of fear. Something told him to slam the door and scurry back to bed. He began to feel that he might have misjudged his own strength. He was not one of those who could investigate the secrets of the other world without coming to harm.

And yet all courage had not abandoned him. He held council with himself, telling himself that the Gen'ral certainly did not intend to lure him into danger. He only wanted to show him where the ring was. If he could only get through the next few minutes he would attain the goal he had been striving toward for years, to return the tired wanderer to his eternal rest.

The Gen'ral had stopped in the middle of the attic to wait for him. Although the light was dimmer here Adrian could still see the dark shape distinctly, with its pleading, outstretched arms. He took courage, crossed the threshold, and they were off once more.

The spirit moved toward the stairs, and when he saw Adrian following he began to descend. He was still moving backwards, and stopped on every step as if to pull the hesitant youth along by his sheer power of will.

They walked slowly, halting often yet never stopped entirely. Adrian tried to keep up his courage by reminding himself how many times he had boasted to his sisters that he would follow the Gen'ral whenever he called. He also reminded himself of how, ever since childhood, he had had a burning desire to explore the unknown and pierce the impenetrable. And now the great moment had come — here he was, following a spirit into the unfamiliar. Would his petty cowardice keep him from finally discovering these secrets?

In this way he forced himself to endure, but he made certain not to approach the spirit too closely. There were always a few arms' lengths between them. When Adrian was on the middle stair, the Gen'ral was at the foot. When Adrian was at the bottom, the Gen'ral was down in the vestibule.

But there Adrian stopped once more. On his right, just by the stairs, was the door to his parents' bedchamber. He touched the doorknob, not intending to open the door, but only to fondle it lovingly. Just think if his parents knew he was outside their door, and in what company! He longed to rush into his mother's arms. He thought that the moment he let the doorknob go he would be putting himself completely at the mercy of the Gen'ral.

While he was standing there with his hand on the doorknob, Adrian saw one of the front doors open and the Gen'ral step across the threshold to go outside.

It had been rather dark both in the attic and on the stairs, but bright light came streaming through the doorway, and it was in that light, for the first time, that Adrian saw the Gen'ral's features.

It was the face of an old man, as he had anticipated. He recognized it very well from the portrait in the drawing room. But his features did not reveal the serenity of death. Instead, there was a look of frenzied craving about him; his mouth formed a terrible grin, confident of triumph and victory.

And this — the discovery of worldly passions reflected in the face of a dead man — was terrifying. Far, far from human desire and suffering do we wish to think of our dear departed as dwelling. We want to imagine them far removed from earthly concerns, completely filled with thoughts of heaven. In this being, still possessed by matters of this world, Adrian felt he was seeing a seducer, an evil spirit, who wanted to lead him to his ruin.

He was overcome with terror. In boundless horror he wrenched open the door of his parents' bedchamber, rushed in and cried:

'Father! Mother! The Gen'ral!'

And at that very moment he fell to the floor in a faint.

The pen falls from my hand. Is it not pointless to try to put this in writing? This story was told to me at twilight by the fireplace. I can still hear the persuasive voice. I feel the proper tingle running down my spine, a tingle not only of fear but also of anticipation.

With what excitement we listened to this particular story because it seemed to lift one corner of the veil concealing all that was unknowable! What a peculiar feeling it left us with, as if a door had been opened, as if something was finally about to emerge from the great unknown.

How much of it is true? It has been handed down from one storyteller to the next, each woman adding or subtracting at will. But doesn't it contain at least a tiny core of truth? Doesn't it give the impression of depicting things that really happened?

The spirit that walked at Hedeby, that was seen in broad daylight, that interfered with the running of the household, that found missing things, who was he, what was he?

Isn't there something uncommonly clear and straightforward about his appearance? Can he not be distinguished from the vast majority of manor house ghosts by virtue of some unique traits? Doesn't it seem as if Miss Spaak really could have heard him throwing apples at the dining room wall, and as if young Baron Adrian really could have followed him through the attic and down the attic steps?

But if so, if so — — — perhaps someone who, even now, can perceive the reality beyond this reality we live in can explain the mystery.

XI

Young Baron Adrian lay tucked into his parents' big bed, pale and immobile. His pulse could still be felt, albeit only very weakly. He had not revived after his deep faint, but the spark of life was not yet extinguished.

There was no physician in Bro parish, so at about four o'clock in the morning one of the farmhands had ridden to Karlstad to try to fetch one. This was a journey of thirty-five miles, and even if the doctor was at home and willing to leave town he could not be expected for at least twelve hours. It was quite possible that a day or more might pass before he arrived.

Baroness Löwensköld sat beside the bed, her eyes fixed on the face of her son. She seemed to think that the feeble spark of life left in him would not be put out if she sat there watching and waiting.

The Baron sometimes sat on the opposite side of the bed, but he was unable to sit still for long. He would take one limp hand between his and feel the pulse, he would walk to the window and gaze down the road, he would take a turn through the house to look at the clock in the drawing room. At these times he would answer the anxious questions he read in the eyes of his daughters and the tutor with a shake of his head and return to the sickbed.

Miss Spaak was the only other person they allowed in there. Not the young Baron's sisters nor any of the maids, only the housekeeper. She knew how to move softly, how to pitch her voice, she was a good person to have near the sickbed.

Miss Spaak had awakened in the middle of the night when Adrian screamed. When she heard the thud that followed she rushed out of bed. She pulled on her clothes, although she could not now remember how. Still, it was one of her rules of wisdom never to run out undressed, because you can do no good that way. In the drawing room she met the Baroness who was on the way to fetch help, and then she and his parents had lifted Adrian into their big four poster bed. At first they all took him for dead, but then Miss Spaak had felt a slight pulsing at one of his wrists.

They had tried to revive him with the usual techniques, but he was very weak indeed, and their every effort only seemed to make his strength wane. They were soon discouraged and afraid to go on. All they could do was to sit and wait.

The Baroness liked having Miss Spaak in the room because she was so calm and so firmly convinced that Adrian soon would recover. She let the housekeeper tend to her, let her comb her hair and put on her shoes. When it was time to put on her dress she had to stand up, but she left the buttoning and tugging to her housekeeper, and never took her eyes from her son's face.

Miss Spaak brought her some coffee and, with gentle insistence, persuaded her to empty the cup.

The Baroness had the feeling that Miss Spaak was in there with her all the time, but she was out in the kitchen too, seeing that the meals were served on schedule. She forgot nothing. She was pale as death, but she performed her tasks. The family's breakfast was ready on time and the boy who tended the cows had his lunch packet when he left for the pasture.

In the kitchen the servants asked what had happened to the young Baron, and Miss Spaak told them that all they knew was that he had come rushing into his parent's bedchamber shouting something about the Gen'ral. Then he had fainted, and now no one could revive him.

'The Gen'ral must've appeared to him,' said the kitchen maid.

'Isn't it strange, though, that he should be so harsh to one of his own?' asked the housemaid.

'Oh well, he must have lost patience with them. They did nought but laugh at him. I suppose he wanted his ring.'

'You don't mean to say you think the ring is here at Hedeby?' said the housemaid. 'He'd burn the house down over our heads to get it back.'

'I'm sure it's in some cranny here somewhere,' said the kitchen maid. 'Why else would he be stalking the place all the time?'

That day Miss Spaak made an exception to her laudable rule of never listening to the servants' gossip about the gentry.

'What's this ring you're talking about?' she asked.

'Don't you know, Miss, that the Gen'ral walks here because he wants his signet ring back?' said the kitchen maid, pleased to have been asked.

She and the housemaid were quick to tell Miss Spaak the story of the grave robbery and the Divine verdict, and when the housekeeper had heard it all, she did not for a moment doubt that the ring had somehow come to Hedeby and was hidden there.

Miss Spaak began to tremble, just as she had the first time she met the Gen'ral on the attic stairs. This was exactly what she had always feared. Now she knew how cruel and merciless this spirit could be. It was clear to her that if the Gen'ral did not get his ring back Baron Adrian would die.

Being a resolute person, as soon as Miss Spaak had drawn this conclusion, she realized what had to be done. If the terrible ring was at Hedeby, it ought to be possible to find it.

She went into the house for a moment, glanced into the bedroom and found things unchanged, ran up the attic stairs and made Adrian's bed so it would be ready if he improved and could be moved there. Then she went in to see the girls and their tutor, who were sitting there so worried they could get nothing done. She told them enough of what she now knew for them to understand what was at stake, and asked them whether they wouldn't be willing to help her look for the ring.

Yes, they were ready and willing. The young mistresses and their tutor said they would search the house, all the rooms and the whole attic. Miss Spaak went out to the kitchen wing personally and put every single maid in the place to work.

'The Gen'ral appears just as often in the kitchen as in the big house,' she thought. 'Something tells me the ring is out here.'

They turned the place inside out, looked everywhere in the kitchen and the larder, the bakery and the brewery. They searched the cracks in the walls and the fireplaces, emptied the spice canisters and even poked into the mouseholes.

And all the while she never forgot to be running across the yard to check on things in the bedchamber. One time she found the Baroness sitting there crying.

'He's worse,' she said. 'I think he's dying.'

Miss Spaak leaned forward, took Adrian's limp hand in hers and felt his pulse.

'No, Baroness,' she said, 'if anything, he is somewhat better.'

She managed to calm her mistress's nerves, but she was close to despair herself. Imagine if the young Baron did not live until she found the ring!

She was so upset that, for one moment, she forgot to watch herself. When she set down Adrian's hand she stroked it just a little. She was hardly aware of it herself, but the Baroness noticed.

'Mon dieu,' she thought, 'poor child! Is that it? Perhaps I should tell her . . . But it is of no account since we are to lose him. He has crossed the Gen'ral, and whoever crosses the Gen'ral must die.'

When Miss Spaak went back out to the kitchen she asked the maids if there wasn't anyone in these parts people sent for at times like this. Was there really nothing they could do before the doctor got there?

Yes, of course, elsewhere people sent for Marit Eriksdotter from Olsby when someone was hurt. She could stop bleeding and put twisted joints right, and she might be able to wake Baron Adrian from the sleep of death, but it was unlikely she'd be willing to come to Hedeby.

When Miss Spaak and the housemaid were speaking of Marit Eriksdotter, the kitchen maid was standing on a stepladder looking up on the high shelf where the missing silver had once been found.

'Oh,' she cried, 'here's something I've been looking for for ages. If it isn't Baron Adrian's old knitted cap!'

Miss Spaak was horrified. What a state things must have been in before her arrival at Hedeby! What could Baron Adrian's cap be doing there?

'It's not as strange as all that,' said the kitchen maid. 'When he outgrew it he gave it to me to make oven gloves from. How lucky I found it!'

Miss Spaak quickly took the cap from her.

'How wasteful to cut it up,' she said. 'Some poor person could make better use of it.'

A few minutes later she took the cap out into the yard and began to beat the dust out of it. While she was doing so, the Baron came out of the big house.

'We think Adrian is worse,' he said.

'Is there no one in these parts who knows about healing?' Miss

Spaak asked him innocently. 'The maids mentioned a woman called Marit Eriksdotter.'

The Baron stiffened.

'It's not that I would hesitate to send for my worst enemy when Adrian's life is at stake,' he said. 'But it would do no good. Marit Eriksdotter won't come to Hedeby.'

Miss Spaak did not dare to contradict him when he put it this way. She went on searching the whole kitchen wing, saw to it that dinner was prepared and that even the Baroness got something into her. The ring had not been found, and Miss Spaak kept saying to herself:

'We must find the ring. The Gen'ral will let Adrian die if we don't find him his ring.'

That afternoon Miss Spaak took a walk over to Olsby. She went on her own authority. The sick man's pulse had been weaker and the beats farther and farther apart every time she had gone into the room. She could not go on waiting for the doctor from Karlstad. She knew it was more than likely that Marit would say no, but Miss Spaak wanted to leave no stone unturned.

Marit Eriksdotter was sitting in her usual place on the steps to her cabin when Miss Spaak came. She had nothing to busy her hands with, but was leaning back, eyes closed. She was not asleep, however, and she looked up when she heard Miss Spaak's footsteps, and recognized her at once.

'Aha,' she said, 'so now they're sending for me to come to Hedeby, are they?'

'Oh, Marit, have you already heard the awful news?' asked Miss Spaak.

'Yes, I've heard about it,' said Marit, 'and I do not want to come.'

Miss Spaak did not say a word in reply. Hopeless despair descended upon her. Nothing had gone her way, and this was the final blow. She could see and hear that Marit was pleased. She had been sitting there on the steps gloating over their misfortune, gloating over the fact that Adrian Löwensköld was going to die.

Up to this point Miss Spaak had managed to keep her chin up. She hadn't screamed and wailed when she saw Adrian Löwensköld lying prone on the floor. All she could think about was to help him, and everyone else. But Marit's resistance broke her will power. She began to cry, hard and uncontrollably. She faltered toward the grey wall of one of the outbuildings, lay her forehead against it, sobbing and sighing.

Marit leaned a little forward. For a long time her eyes were fixed on the unfortunate girl. 'Oh, is that it?' she thought.

And as Marit sat watching someone weep tears of love over the one she held dear, something happened in her own heart.

A few hours earlier she had heard that the Gen'ral had appeared to Adrian and virtually frightened him to death, and she had said to herself that her hour of revenge had come at last. She had awaited it for many years, but always in vain. Captain Löwensköld had gone to the grave without getting his punishment. Although the Gen'ral had been walking at Hedeby again ever since the time she'd seen to it that the ring was returned, it had looked as if he couldn't pursue his own family with the heartlessness for which he was infamous.

But now misfortune was upon them, and who did they turn to for help but herself? They might as well go to the men who died on the gallows.

It did her good to say: 'I won't come.' It was her way of getting revenge.

But when Marit saw the young girl stand there crying, leaning her head against the wall, a memory awakened in her. 'I, too, have stood crying like that, leaning against a hard wall, when there was no one to turn to for support.'

And all at once the love Marit had felt when she was young welled up inside her and flowed hot in her veins. Surprised, she sat thinking:

'That was how I felt in those days. That was how it felt to care for someone. That's the kind of wonderful, strong feeling it was.'

She could see him with her inner eye, the young, happy, strong, handsome Paul Eliasson. She recalled the look in his eyes, his voice, his every gesture. Her whole heart was filled with him.

Marit believed she had loved him all the time, and no doubt she had. But how her feelings had cooled over the long years! For a moment the passion in her heart was rekindled with its bright intensity.

And as her love reawakened so did the memory of the terrible pain it causes to lose the one you love.

Marit looked over at Miss Spaak, who was still standing there sobbing. Now Marit knew what she was feeling. Before, the chill of passing time had been upon her. She had forgotten how the fire can burn, but now she remembered. She refused to cause anyone else to suffer as she had, so she rose and approached the housekeeper.

'Come along, Miss. I shall go with you,' she said brusquely.

And so it was that Miss Spaak returned to Hedeby in the company of Marit Eriksdotter. All the way there Marit had said not a word. Afterwards, Miss Spaak understood that she had been walking along thinking over how to go about finding the ring.

The housekeeper walked Marit right up to the front door and showed her into the bedchamber. There, all was as before. Adrian lay handsome and pale, but still as death, and the Baroness sat watching over him, motionless. She did not look up until Marit Eriksdotter approached the bed.

The very instant she recognized the woman who stood looking at her son, she sank to the floor at her feet, her face against her skirts.

'Marit, Marit!' she said. 'Please don't think about all the harm the Löwenskölds have done you. Help him, Marit! Help him!'

The farm woman drew back, but Adrian's desperate mother followed her, on her knees.

'You have no idea how frightened I have been ever since the Gen'ral began to haunt this place. I have been living and waiting in dread. I knew that now his wrath would be turned on us.'

Marit stood motionless. She shut her eyes and seemed to withdraw into herself. Miss Spaak was positive it pleased her to hear the Baroness speak of her suffering.

'I have wanted to approach you, Marit, and go down on my knees to you as I do now, and beg you to forgive the Löwenskölds. But I have not dared. I believed it was impossible for you to forgive.'

'You mustn't ask that of me, Baroness,' said Marit, 'for it is true, I cannot forgive.'

'And yet you are here?'

'I have come for the sake of your housekeeper, because she asked me to.'

With these words Marit walked to the other side of the four poster. She placed a hand on the sick man's chest and mumbled a few words. She also knit her brow, lifted her eyebrows and puckered her mouth. To Miss Spaak she seemed to be doing exactly as healing women always did.

'I think he will live,' said Marit, 'but you must remember, Baroness, that it is for the young woman's sake, and hers alone, that I shall help him.'

'Yes, Marit,' said the Baroness, 'I shall remember it forever.'

It seemed to Miss Spaak that her mistress had wanted to add something, but she cut her words short and pursed her lips.

'And now, Baroness, you must permit me to do as I see fit.'

'You may have an absolutely free hand, Marit. The Baron is not in. I asked him to ride to meet the doctor and hurry him along.'

Miss Spaak had anticipated Marit Eriksdotter's making some

kind of effort to rouse the young Baron from his state, but to her great disappointment she did nothing of the sort.

Instead, Marit demanded to have every piece of Baron Adrian's clothing gathered together, both the garments he wore nowadays and whatever of his old clothing might still be around. She wanted to see everything he had ever worn, from stockings and shirts to mittens and caps.

That day no one at Hedeby did anything but search. Although Miss Spaak sighed over Marit's being nothing but a run of the mill healing woman with the usual tricks, she searched every chest and attic space, every cupboard and wardrobe, to find everything the sick man had owned. The young mistresses, who knew most everything about what Adrian had worn, helped her, and she soon brought a whole pile of clothing down to Marit.

Marit spread out the clothes on the kitchen table and examined each garment with care. She set aside one old pair of shoes, a pair of small mittens and a shirt. All the while she muttered, in an endless monotone:

'One pair for his feet, one pair for his hands, one thing for his body and one for his head.

'I need something for his head,' she suddenly said in her normal voice. 'I need something soft and warm.'

Miss Spaak showed her the hats and other headgear she had found.

'No, I need something soft and warm,' said Marit. 'Didn't Baron Adrian have a knitted cap like other boys?'

Miss Spaak was about to say that she hadn't seen one, but the kitchen maid anticipated her:

'Don't you remember? I found his old knitted cap this morning, but you took it away from me, Miss.'

And thus Miss Spaak was forced to bring out the knitted cap she had determined never to part with, that she had planned to cherish to the end of her days.

Once Marit had the cap, she began her incantation again, but her tone of voice had changed. She sounded like a cat, purring with satisfaction.

'Now', said Marit, when she had stood muttering over the cap, turning and twisting it for a long time. 'Now I have everything I need. It will all have to be put into the Gen'ral's grave.'

But when Miss Spaak heard this, she grew quite desperate.

'Marit, how could you imagine the Captain would have the vault opened to put these old rags in?' she asked.

Marit looked at her with a trace of a smile. Taking Miss Spaak by the hand she drew her over to a window, so their backs were to everyone else in the kitchen. Then she held Adrian's cap up before Miss Spaak's eyes and separated the strands of yarn in the big tassel.

She said not a word, nor did Miss Spaak, but when the housekeeper turned back toward the room she was pale as death, and her hands were trembling.

Marit made a little bundle of the garments she had chosen and turned them over to Miss Spaak.

'Now I have done what I can,' she said. 'Now it is up to the rest of you to see to it that these things are put into the grave.'

And with that she departed.

*

Miss Spaak was walking in the direction of the churchyard just after ten o'clock in the evening. She had taken Marit's little bundle, but otherwise she was walking entirely at random. She hadn't the slightest idea of how she could get the things down into the grave.

Baron Löwensköld had come riding in the company of the doctor just after Marit had gone, and the housekeeper had hoped that the Doctor would be able to bring Adrian back to life without her having to take further action. But the doctor had declared at once that he was powerless. He said that the young man had no more than a few hours left to live.

So Miss Spaak had taken the bundle under her arm and gone off. She knew there was no possibility of inducing the Baron to have the gravestones lifted and the mortared-up vault opened just to put in some of Baron Adrian's old clothes.

If she told him what was really in the bundle, she was certain he would return the ring to its rightful owner at once, but to do this she would have to betray Marit Eriksdotter.

She had no doubt that it was Marit who, some time back, had returned the ring to Hedeby. Baron Adrian had said something about Marit once having mended his cap. No, Miss Spaak couldn't let the Baron see the matter in its proper light.

Afterwards, Miss Spaak thought how odd it was that she had felt no fear that night. But she stepped over the low churchyard wall and approached the Löwensköld grave without thinking of anything but how she was ever going to get the ring into it.

She sat down on the gravestone and clasped her hands in prayer. 'If God does not help me now,' she thought, 'this grave will surely be opened, and not for this ring, but for someone I will forever mourn.'

In the middle of her prayer Miss Spaak noticed a tiny movement in the grass growing around the headstone on the grave . A little head peeped out, but it vanished when Miss Spaak gave a start. For she was as frightened of mice as mice were of her. But the sight of that mouse gave Miss Spaak a sudden inspiration. She rushed over to a big lilac, broke off a long dead branch and stuck it into the mousehole.

To begin with she stuck it straight down, but encountered immediate resistance. So she tried poking it down at an angle, and it went straight in, down toward the vault. She was surprised at how deeply it penetrated. The whole switch vanished. She pulled it quickly up again, and measured its length against her arm. It was six feet long, and had been extended down in its entirety. The switch must have reached into the vault.

Never in all her life had Miss Spaak kept her wits about her so well. She realized the mice must have tunnelled their way into the vault. They could have found a little duct, or some of the masonry might have eroded.

She lay down on the ground, pulled up a tuft of grass, dug away the loose earth and stuck down her arm. She could reach down unobstructed, but her arm was not long enough to touch the brickwork.

So she hastily untied her bundle and took out the cap. She attached it to the switch and tried to angle it slowly into the hole. It quickly vanished. She continued to manoeuvre the switch slowly and carefully, farther and farther down. All at once, when almost the whole switch was below ground, she felt it being snatched from her hand with a jerk.

Although it was possible that it had simply fallen from its own weight, she was absolutely certain it had been pulled from her.

Then, at last, she was scared. She stuffed everything else from the bundle into the hole, replaced the earth and the tuft as neatly as she could, and ran. She did not walk a step, but ran all the way to Hedeby.

When she got to the yard both the Baron and the Baroness were standing on the front steps. They approached her eagerly.

'Miss Spaak, wherever have you been?' they asked her. 'We've been waiting for you.'

'Is Baron Adrian dead?' Miss Spaak asked.

'No, he's not dead,' said the Baron. 'But won't you please tell us where you have been?'

Miss Spaak was so short of breath she could hardly speak, but she told them of the mission Marit had assigned to her, and that she had managed to get at least one of the articles down into the vault through a mouse hole.

'This is most remarkable indeed, Miss Spaak,' said the Baron, 'for Adrian is truly better. He awoke a little while ago, and his first words were: "Now the Gen'ral has the ring." '

'His heart is beating normally again,' said the Baroness, 'and he insists on speaking with you, Miss Spaak. He says you are the one who has saved his life.'

They permitted Miss Spaak to go in to see Adrian alone. He was sitting up in bed and when he saw her he opened his arms.

'I know, I already know!' he cried. 'The Gen'ral has the ring, and it was all your doing, Miss Spaak.'

Miss Spaak was laughing and crying in his embrace, and he kissed her on the brow.

'I have you to thank for my life,' he said. 'I would be dead and gone at this very moment if it weren't for you. I will never be able to thank you enough.'

The rapturous tone with which the young man had welcomed her may have made the unfortunate Miss Spaak remain too long in his arms. He hastened to add:

'And I am not the only one who has you to thank, Miss Spaak. There is another as well.'

He showed her the locket he was wearing. Through her tears, Miss Spaak discerned a miniature of a young woman.

'You are the first person, Miss Spaak, beside my parents, to hear the news,' he said. 'When she comes to Hedeby in a few weeks' time, she will thank you far better than I can.'

So Miss Spaak curtsied to the young Baron to thank him for having confided in her. She would have liked to tell him that she had no intention of staying at Hedeby to receive his fiancée. But she caught herself in time. A poor girl must think twice before she gives up a good place.

Afterword

Beneath a guise of ultimate respectability, Selma Lagerlöf has always been a highly controversial author, and she is likely to remain so. Initially, the disguise was self-imposed: hidden deep inside the spinster schoolmistress who was a great teller of tales but no threat to the male literary establishment, was one of the mothers of contemporary Swedish women's literature. Although, in 1909, she was the first woman (and the first Swedish author) ever to become the Nobel laureate for literature, there were then and still are critics and reviewers who have marginalized her writing as trivial.

At the time, her denigrators claimed that Lagerlöf received the prize by default — it was simply a way for the Swedish Academy of Arts and Letters to be able to award it to a Swedish author and yet not to August Strindberg. Today, while Selma Lagerlöf's books have among the highest public library circulation in Sweden and are the object of new literary criticism being written both by Swedish scholars and academics abroad, they are still trivialized and marginalized by others. Take, for example, the latest history of Swedish literature (eds. Lars Lönnroth and Sven Delblanc, four volumes to date) in which Selma Lagerlöf 'barely passes inspection' (Professor Thure Stenström, *Svenska Dagbladet*, arts page, 21 April 1989).

The Löwensköld Ring was published in 1925, and in English translation in 1928. Not only is the original still in print in Swedish, but it is available in a popular cheap press paperback edition. The original English translation was never reprinted. Now, sixty-five years after its publication and fifty years after Selma Lagerlöf's death, Norvik Press presents a timely new translation.

The Löwensköld Ring is an exciting novella in several senses. As is true of much of Selma Lagerlöf's production, it can easily be read at the superficial level, in this case as a spellbinding tale of ghosts and murder. Yet the whodunit is not the only genre classification into which *The Löwensköld Ring* may be slotted — it can equally well be considered and early feminist work, a psychological novella, or a metafictional narrative. Furthermore, the excitement deepens if the reader is able to dive beneath the surface and study this work as a masterpiece of literary and psychological ambiguity. In that sense, *The Löwensköld Ring* has features in common with Henry James's *The Turn of the Screw*.

In the *TLS* of 28 August 1987, Roy Harris, Professor of General Linguistics at Oxford, addresses the subject of the ephemerality of literary translation, referring to translation as 'a point of contact between one synchronic cultural system and another'. He argues that the fact that the post-structuralist period of the twentieth century has seen a major shift from a mimetic to an analytic conception of the arts makes a strong case for frequent retranslation of literary classics, based in a new way on a contemporary, structurally coherent analysis of the original. It is not on the grounds of errors of representation that translations should be condemned. The worst possible fault of a translator today, he says, is failure 'to present any structurally coherent analysis at all'.

Despite the fact that Selma Lagerlöf's literary texts are still the subject of considerable debate in Sweden today, they have hardly been retranslated into English at all. The present text is an attempt to carry out what Harris calls 'the diagnostic undertaking of the translator', to bring the text of *The Löwensköld Ring* up to date for the English language reader, and to show its concern with the practical, with what Martha Nussbaum refers to as 'the ethical and social questions that give literature its high importance in our lives'. As a contemporary translation, it will also be ephemeral rather than definitive. Its aim is to underline the relevance of Lagerlöf's early twentieth century writing for the late twentieth century reader.

Although it is a complete story in itself, *The Löwensköld Ring* is actually the first volume of a trilogy including *The Löwensköld Ring*, *Charlotte Löwensköld*, and *Anna Svärd*. These books comprise Selma Lagerlöf's last strictly fictional production, her final works being more autobiographical in nature. Brigitta Holm has interestingly demonstrated how the Löwensköld trilogy also brings Lagerlöf's fictional world full circle, returning to and tying up thematic loose ends running through her works from the opening paragraph of her first novel, *Gösta Berlings saga* (*Gösta Berling's Saga*, 1891). In terms of imagery, too, it is also of interest to acknowledge that the circular, endless ring dominates the title of the lead volume of the trilogy, and that the final chapter of the concluding volume is entitled 'Vigselringen' — 'The Wedding Ring'.

A stream of ambiguity runs very deep in *The Löwensköld Ring*. The superficial simplicity of the story itself belies layer upon layer of complexity. Question after question emerges, usually to be answered in at least two apparently mutually exclusive but fully possible ways, leaving the reader uncomfortably uncertain of what he is 'supposed' to think. In his *Philosophy of Rhetoric*, I.A. Richards wrote of ambiguity as 'an inevitable consequence of the powers of language' and warned his readers of the dangers of the simplification of literal expression. In various ways, the first translation of *The Löwensköld Ring* was extraordinarily literal, but this short and seemingly straightforward piece of literature can also be strenuous and demanding, going round and round in circles, in rings.

Stepping into the very opening of this novella is like entering a circular argument, walking into a room where a heated conversation is under way, rather than being present as a story begins. The first-person narrator begins with a defensive response to a question or statement the reader has not heard. 'Of course I know, I know just as well as you do, what things used to be like', she says to her unidentified partner in dialogue. 'That's exactly the point of the story I'm about to tell you.'

Looking back over Selma Lagerlöf's fiction, Professor Vivi Edström has noted that the first-person narrator has been conspicuously absent since her very first novel, *Gösta Berling's Saga*. Although the narrator of *The Löwensköld Ring* does not appear in person in every chapter, her voice is an important one.

Chapter I provides the narrative framework for the story, describing the Löwensköld ring of the title as it appears in a portrait. But this ostensibly realistic description of a full-size painting is also the first manifestation of a tension between appearance and reality, of the ambiguity that permeates the novella. At first glance, says the narrator, anyone would take the portrait to be of King Karl XII, but upon closer examination it proves instead to be the image of General Bengt Löwensköld, humble and devoted servant of that very king he resembles. The most outstanding item in the portrait is the ring, given General Löwensköld by King Karl, which he bore with great pride in life as in death, in reality as in the painting. Virtually every sentence in this chapter reinforces the vacillation between what the narrator implies that the reader might believe and what was the case. After the initial discussion of belief in the supernatural versus rejection of superstition and the description of the portrait that resembles the King but is the General, there is a discussion of whether it was egotistical vanity or humility and devotion that prompted the General to refuse to be parted from his ring at death. The question of whether the villagers attending the General's funeral resented or admired his sons for their decision to abide by that wish is also raised. The chapter concludes with a paragraph portraying the impossibility of stealing the ring, in a way that makes it clear to the reader that the ring is indeed likely to be stolen. Thus is the stage of uncertainty craftfully set.

In Chapter II the theft takes place, almost as if by accident — and at whose instigation? The act is committed by a man and his wife, and the narrative build-up is at once almost farcical and deeply piercing. Very few words are exchanged between Bård Bårdsson and his wife, and the little that is said often appears to be misunderstood. Nothing is explicitly agreed upon, yet the damage is done. Has Bård Bårdsson's wife (never referred to by any other name than 'she', 'her', and 'his wife' despite her prominent role) manipulated him into committing the theft she finds so enticing, done her best to save him from his own evil temptation, or been an equal partner in crime? Do these two understand one another so well that the verbal exchanges are almost superfluous, or do they suffer from a fundamental inability to communicate? Do Bård and his wife know, individually, what they want to do, or is each led on by a desire to please the other?

The fundamental contradiction between what is and what appears to be, portrayed at a general level in Chapter I, is thus intensified at the individual level in Chapter II. At the end of Chapter II the couple is walking home from the graveyard, feeling a consensus of satisfaction with their night's work when, at the eastern horizon, they see their homestead in flames. Imagery of fire, and the deeper significance of its good and evil sides, is picked up by the narrator in Chapter VII.

Chapter III lifts the reader from the specific to an even higher level of generality than in Chapter I — the religious and the mythical. The first-person narrator returns (having been absent in Chapter II), saying she is moved to interject a little story about King Karl's reception when, one Sunday, he made an unexpected visit to a rural church, entering when the service was in progress.

She explains that she is trying to understand two apparent contradictions, that the people at once loved this king gently and feared him terribly, and that they could believe that he was so strong as to be able to confer upon General Bengt Löwensköld the power with which to defend his ownership of the King's ring even after both their deaths. For no one, she says, was at all surprised to find that he had this power, and exacted his retribution for the theft. This chapter, again, leaves the reader hanging in terms of what the narrator is 'actually' saying: is the twentieth century reader 'supposed' to see through the myths and rituals that apparently duped the nineteenth century villagers of Värmland, or to look deep inside and acknowledge the primitive nature of our own reactions, realize that we, too, would probably rise in the presence of a king we despised, and fully expect the dead General to revenge his plundered grave, or neither or both?

In the next couple of chapters the narrator is invisible, and we readers are left largely to our own devices in terms of these larger issues while being thrown headlong into the heart of the story of the 'possessed' ring. Years have passed as Chapter IV opens, and Bård Bårdsson is on his deathbed. Since the theft of the ring, he has led a totally lonely life of Job-like trials and tribulations, and now wants to repent before he dies. We readers sit outside his cottage with his daughter, perched on a stony outcrop, listening to her brother's summary as he eavesdrops on his father's confession to the parson. Events become narrative, through distance and time, and through telling from mouth to ear to mouth, edited at each step of the way. Was there ever one true version of these events?

The ring changes hands — Bård gives it to the parson, his son steals it back and then dies or is murdered as the ring moves on — it is either stolen or taken accidentally — into the hands of one Paul Eliasson. Paul, his foster father and foster brother all subsequently lose their lives for this 'theft', which they consistently claim that they were unaware of and innocent of having committed. Yet the sole item they bequeath to their survivor, Paul's fiancée Marit Eriksson, the daughter of his foster father Erik, is a garment in which the ring is concealed. Could this possibly be coincidental? Is there ever any such thing as coincidence? Was anyone responsible?

All these turns of event are couched in very carefully formulated language. Unfortunately, the 1928 translation contains a serious (and interesting) translation error at a vital moment, which distorts the reader's perception of the honesty of one of the main characters in the story. The three men are deep in the forest, being questioned by a vigilante posse led by General Löwensköld's son about their possible theft of the ring. Löwensköld is becoming increasingly desperate to find a reason to exact his revenge on these men, and he asks Ivar Ivarsson, the brother, whether a leather pouch that has been found amongst his possessions belongs to him. The Swedish text then reads (my italics throughout) :

Om nu Ivar Ivarsson hade svarat ja, *skulle saken kanske därmed varit slut, men i stället erkände han med största lugn i världen.*
-- Nej, den låg på stigen långt ifrån det stället, där Ingilbert föll.

The 1928 text reads:

Now had Ivar answered 'yes', *the matter would have ended, but, instead, he gave utterance to the most frightful lie.*
'No, it was lying on the path, not far from the place where Ingilbert fell'.

This meaningful error has been rectified in the new translation,

111

where the passage reads:

> If Ivar Ivarsson had simply answered yes *that might have been the end of the matter, but instead he made an admission, as calmly as could be.*
> 'No, it was on the path not far from where Ingilbert fell'.

What makes this error especially interesting in addition to the matter of the reader's perception of Ivar Ivarsson's credibility, is both the fact that the narrative indication of indeterminacy, 'kanske' was lost in the 1928 translation and that it may be the case that the translator, whose knowledge of Swedish appears perfectly competent in the vast majority of cases, has somehow confused 'lögn' (lie) with 'lugn' (calm). One question which arises is whether this has occurred because the translator, either consciously or unconsciously. has simply assumed that Ivar Ivarsson is guilty and lying. Although the words may be ortho-graphically similar enough for it to be possible to chalk the matter up to a moment of slipped attentiveness on the part of the translator, the thematic context belies this possibility, as the sentence also contains the word 'erkände', admitted, and it is syntactically difficult to reconcile admitting with lying. The main issue for the reader, however, is that, no matter why or how it has occurred, the story line has been obscured, and the subsequent events, shrouded in uncertainty even in the original, unnecessarily confused.

At the actual physical middle of the story and at its thematic core as well, is a scene, depicted with masterful subtlety and irony, which epitomizes all the previous innuendos with regard to our human difficulty in claiming responsibility for our actions, and accepting the extent to which we determine our own fate.

The three men have been acquitted of the charges of robbery and murder in a lower court, but that judgement has been appealed against by the General's family. The men are respectable farmers (although Paul was born in Russia, which makes him considerably more suspect), but the General's family is more or less considered locally to be on a par with His Majesty King Frederik who in turn is only second to the Almighty. The ring has been missing for years, and although Bård Bårdsson has suffered, no one has been duly blamed and punished for the crime. But neither the court nor the present King can comfortably determine whom to convict. And so: '. . . a Divine judgement was to settle the case. At the next court session, in the presence of the judge, the jury and the general public, the accused parties were to play dice. The man who cast the lowest roll would then be considered guilty and be condemned unto death by hanging for his crime while the other two would be set free to return to their everyday lives.'

This seems simple enough, almost an easy way out. But what happens? Uncertainty prevails, and not even the patterns of dots on the 'neutral' dice are able to determine who is guilty. Although, it is, in fact, far from clear that any one of them has committed the crime in question, all three men lose their lives.

Thirty years then pass, and the narrative resumes as Marit Eriksdotter, the late Paul Eliasson's fiancée whose love for him has stayed with her all the time, sits wanting to knit something pretty, but is unable to call to mind a pattern. Looking for inspiration in a long-unopened chest, she finds, to her shock and dismay, the very ring she has steadfastly spent years believing the man innocent of stealing. When she stumbles over the ring, she asks herself: ' Could she ever imagine that Paul would have sent her the cap to remember him by if he had known it concealed the stolen goods?' In wondering this at all, of course, she *has* already

113

imagined that very possibility, and yet she answers herself, immediately with: 'No, if one thing was certain in this world, it was this: he had not known that the ring worn on a dead man's finger, was hidden in the cap.' For the reader the ultimate sense of all things' ambiguity lies here: since Marit can only speculate and may very well be wrong, the one clear truth is that *nothing in this world is certain!*

The rest of the novella is dominated by this striking theme: the search for patterns to explain life, our dismay when the patterns we evolve prove false, and our ability to adapt, adjust our patterns and go on. The theme sets the tone for the two other books of the trilogy as well, for although the General's ring does eventually come to rest, Marit never makes her peace with the arbitrary execution of her loved ones, and her story, her experience, appears to determine the fate of other Löwensölds, from generation to generation.

This novella, and the entire trilogy can, similarly, be read as Lagerlöf's final attempt to make peace, in her fiction, with her own concept of herself as an author and her variable status in the predominantly male literary establishment. Another character in *The Löwensköld Ring*, instrumental in the resolution of the mystery of the ring itself, is Malvina Spaak, the Löwensköld's housekeeper. Skilled at her profession, and essential to the home but only an employed staff member, she may serve as a vehicle for Lagerlöf to make succinct metafictional comments about her own status as an author in the contemporary writing community.

Malvina accepts her job without being informed of the fact that the house is haunted, and she is actually terrified of ghosts. When her employer, the Baroness, lets her in on something of the family secret, she accepts her fate, knowing that 'a poor girl must really think twice before she gives up a good place'. Malvina would do almost anything to retain her 'good place', and like Selma Lagerlöf, she proves to be marvellous at her job, carrying out her duties to everyone's great satisfaction. She is even permitted to have dinner at table with the gentry, and is considered an asset to the establishment despite her background. Still, and again like Lagerlöf, as soon as things do not run exactly like clockwork she is relegated firmly back to her place, and she is always frightened of losing her job. The narrator, too, despairs towards the end of the book of the possibility of her undertaking, making the (women's) oral tradition into conventional (male-dominated) literature. At the climax of the tale, she burst out: 'The pen falls from my hand. Is it not pointless to try to put this in writing? This story was told to me at twilight by the fireplace. I can still hear the persuasive voice.' And although, in the end, it is Malvina who makes the renewal of the Löwensköld family possible at all, as Lagerlöf certainly contributed to the renewal of Swedish literature, she is simultaneously left painfully aware of her station.

There is considerable biographical indication that Lagerlöf, late in life, felt her work to be only marginally accepted into the Swedish literary canon. The novella ends with great disappointment for Malvina when the pattern she had hoped for her life proves to be impossible to realize, and an almost verbatim repetition of her earlier decision, uttered with a vast sense of resignation (and possibly meant to be read with a sense of humour or ironic distance): 'A poor girl must think twice before she gives up a good place.' It is interesting to note in this context, and in the confirmation of the necessity of new translations of classic works, the 1928 translation, although not factually incorrect on this point, deprives the statement of all possible feminist overtones and also greatly dilutes its class consciousness implications, as well as making the possible association to Lagerlöf's own career as a writer more difficult. Both occurrences are translated as: 'beggars cannot be choosers'.

Another interesting error in the 1928 translation may further indicate the translator's own interpretation of the characters' personalities, despite linguistic indications to the contrary. The narrator describes Miss Spaak's sceptical attitude towards the nonchalance with which the ghost is treated, saying that she:

anade från första stund, att det skulle ta en ända med förkräckelse.

The 1928 translation renders this line as:

and from the very first she determined to try and conquer her terror.

The new translation reads:

and she suspected from the start that something dreadful would come of it.

Miss Spaak *does* act very bravely in relation to the ghost, but surely it is important for the English language reader to have access to the Swedish narrative comment that she anticipates an awful turn of events. Perhaps, however, the 1928 translator who, as we have seen, conceived of the honest Ivar Ivarsson as a liar, also saw Malvina Spaak (and if Spaak *is* a vehicle for metafictional comment, perhaps the translator saw Lagerlöf herself) in the traditional woman's role of forcing herself to adapt to her surroundings rather than standing up for her own opinion and feelings!

Although a translation inevitably implies losses, it is my hope that the reader of this text will have access to at least some of its potential. In his article on the ephemerality of translation referred to above, Roy Harris states that a translation 'has no claim for validity other than as a historical statement, and like all historical statements it is intrinsically provisional, corrigible and replace-able'. This translation stands as a late twentieth-century attempt to keep Selma Lagerlöf as readable in English as she is in Swedish, in an attempt to improve Lagerlöf's chances of keeping her place in the canon of world literature. Presumably, it will be corrected and replaced when history so requires. Today, the story of the ring contains, among other things a herstory, a mystery, a social commentary, a statement on women's writing and a love story. Readers of translations are also, unfortunately, beggars who cannot often be choosers, but it is my aspiration to have provided the readers of this story with at least some range of choice.

OCTOBER 1990   L.S.